MESMERIZING MOMENT

Kate looked into the stranger's eyes, and everything else dwindled to insignificance. Kate was at a loss to decide exactly what color they were. Amber? They were certainly paler than brown, but she suspected that in some lights, some moods, they might turn to the tawny gold of a cat's eyes. . . .

She became aware that the eyes in question were reciprocating her scrutiny, and she could feel the pulses racing in her neck, leaping in her wrists. This was the most attractive man she had ever encountered.

Unfortunately, he was not the man whom Kate stood to gain all by wedding. He was the one whom she could lose everything by loving. . . .

Though her college majors were history and French. DIANA CAMPBELL worked in the computer industry for a number of years and has written extensively about various aspects of data processing. She had published eighteen short stories and two mystery novels before undertaking her first Regency romance.

THE
LATE
LORD
LATIMER

by
Diana Campbell

A SIGNET BOOK

NEW AMERICAN LIBRARY

Copyright © 1988 by Diana Campbell

SIGNET TRADEMARK REG. U.S. PAT. OFF. AND FOREIGN COUNTRIES
REGISTERED TRADEMARK—MARCA REGISTRADA
HECHO EN CHICAGO, U.S.A.

SIGNET, SIGNET CLASSIC, MENTOR, ONYX, PLUME,
MERIDIAN and NAL BOOKS are published by
NAL PENGUIN INC., 1633 Broadway, New York,
New York 10019

First Printing, November, 1988

1 2 3 4 5 6 7 8 9

PRINTED IN THE UNITED STATES OF AMERICA

1

"Good evening, Miss Morrow." Mr. Barnes, the innkeeper, stepped to Kate's side. "I fear there's but one table left, a small one next to the window. Will that be satisfactory?"

In point of fact, the last place Kate wished to sit was beside a window; she had seen quite enough of the incessant rain these three days past. But as Mr. Barnes had indicated, the dining room was full, and she fancied she had little choice if she wanted to eat. She nodded, and the plump landlord ushered her forward.

"What a storm!" he remarked as they threaded their way among the crowded tables. "Three days already, and it shows no sign of ending."

He shook his head, but Kate noted that his tone was one of considerable cheer. As well it should be, she thought darkly, for Mr. Barnes was one of the few people in Bermuda who stood to profit by the inclement weather. Several ships had managed to limp into St. George's harbor despite the storm, but none had been bold enough to leave port in the howling wind and driving rain. As a consequence, the Palmetto was filled to overflowing with seamen, passengers whose journeys had been interrupted, and prospective passengers—like Kate—whose departures had been delayed.

"Here we are then." Mr. Barnes drew a chair away from the table, and Kate sank into it. "If I may make a recommendation, the grouper is very good this evening."

He had recommended grouper the previous two evenings as well, and Kate strongly suspected that this was the only entrée the Palmetto presently had to offer. Which was no reflection on Mr. Barnes's establishment. Indeed, Kate sometimes marveled that the residents of Bermuda did not develop fins and gills shortly after they were weaned because from that day forward, the only food they could absolutely rely on was fish. There were often shortages of meat and vegetables, even of flour, but the island never lacked for seafood.

"Yes," she murmured, "the grouper would be fine."

Mr. Barnes bobbed his head and bustled away, and Kate gazed out the window. The innkeeper's happy words to the contrary, she believed the storm was beginning to abate. The sky had lightened from black to gray, the furious, blowing rain had decreased to a mere downpour, and for the first time since her arrival at the Palmetto, she could make out the new town hall across King's Square and the nearby spires of St. Peter's Church. Even as she watched, the sky brightened a bit more, and she caught a glimpse of the ships anchored in the harbor. If the weather continued to improve at this rate, the *Queen Anne* would probably sail tomorrow.

Tomorrow. Kate felt a familiar stab of panic, and she hastily averted her eyes from the window. She had been born and brought up in Bermuda, and for as long as she could remember, she had dreamed of going to England. As a child, she had merely wished to visit her parents' homeland and view the wonderful sights they'd mentioned, but later—after Mama and Papa died and she recognized the limited opportunities in Bermuda

—she began to dream of permanently settling in the mother country. If only she had a thousand pounds! she would think. Well, perhaps it would require more than that, but not much more. With two or three thousand pounds, she could travel to England, reclaim her rightful place in society, meet and marry a fine gentleman . . .

But Kate didn't have sixpence to scratch with, much less several thousand pounds, and she resigned herself to a life of genteel servitude on the remote island of her birth. Until—by a stroke of fortune that was little short of miraculous—she had inherited a sum far in excess of her wildest imaginings. As soon as Mrs. Todhunter's estate was settled, Kate had rushed to St. George's and booked passage on the next ship to Plymouth; and if the *Queen Anne* had departed on schedule, she would be well on her way by now.

But the *Queen Anne* was still anchored in the harbor, and the delay had compelled Kate to reexamine her ambitious dream. Her stomach fluttered again, and she dropped her eyes to the worn tablecloth. She had interpreted her unexpected legacy as a miracle; might the storm be a miracle of a different sort? Perhaps fate had been kind enough to warn her that a green-headed colonial would not be accepted in British society regardless of her circumstances. Maybe she should stay in Bermuda after all—

"Kitty?"

The voice had scarcely penetrated Kate's reverie when a hand clamped on her shoulder, and she started and glanced up. Her parents had called her Kitty when she was small, but at the advanced age of ten—fancying herself quite grown up—Kate had insisted that her nickname be changed. She briefly wondered if this was someone who had known her before the transformation: before

Mama died and Papa removed himself and his
young daughter from St. George's to Hamilton.
The man peering down at her was about sixty, she
judged, and might well have been acquainted with
her father. But she was sure, upon consideration,
that she herself had never met him. His hair could
have grayed in the dozen years since she had left
St. George's, but she would have remembered his
remarkable eyes, which were very large and so
dark a brown that they might more accurately be
described as black.

"Forgive me."

The man snatched his hand from Kate's
shoulder and began to fan his face. He was quite
flushed, she noted, and when she discreetly
lowered her gaze, she further observed that he
was much too heavy. His rotund belly created a
substantial gap between the bottom of his waistcoat and the top of his pantaloons, and the seams
of the latter threatened to burst at any moment.

"Forgive me," he repeated.

Kate hastily redirected her attention to his face
and calculated, in the process, that he was considerably above the average in height.

"From the rear," he continued, "you bear an
astonishing resemblance to my daughter Kitty.
Your hair is precisely the same shade of blond as
hers. From the front, of course . . ." He paused and
tilted his head. "Actually, you look quite like Kitty
from the front as well. Though her face is a little
rounder."

Everyone's face was rounder than hers, Kate
thought wryly. When she had grown old enough to
perceive that her cheekbones were unusually
prominent, her cheeks rather too hollow, her chin
distinctly pointed, she had studied the few family
portraits Papa and Mama had brought from
England; but she had not been able to identify the

guilty ancestor responsible for her peculiar features. At least, she comforted herself, she had been blessed with Mama's heart-shaped mouth and Papa's splendid teeth. And—another mystery of inheritance—her eyes were a lovely shade of—

"And my daughter's eyes are green," the man said. "Whereas yours are . . ." His voice trailed off, and he cocked his head again.

Kate liked to think that her eyes were aquamarine, but she had never had the courage to express this opinion aloud. "Blue-green," she supplied.

"Blue-green." He nodded. "May I join you?"

Kate hesitated. Though the man, by his own admission, was old enough to be her father, the difference in their ages did not preclude the possibility of an improper advance. As she debated, Mr. Barnes bounded up to the table, wringing his hands with dismay.

"Mr. Sinclair," the innkeeper panted. "It's always a pleasure to serve you, sir, but as you can see for yourself, the dining room is full." He waved apologetically around. "Perhaps Miss Morrow would permit you to share her table."

Sinclair? Kate silently echoed. She knew of only one Sinclair in Bermuda, and Mr. Barnes's deferential attitude suggested that this was he: Robert Sinclair, reputed to be among the wealthiest men in the colony. She became aware that both Mr. Sinclair and Mr. Barnes were gazing questioningly down at her.

"Yes," she said. "Mr. Sinclair may share my table."

"Very good. I'll bring you a glass of brandy, sir."

The landlord trotted away, and Mr. Sinclair lowered his vast bulk into the chair across from Kate's. It was no easy task: he squirmed about for a full minute before he was able to find a comfortable position, and even then, his enormous belly was firmly jammed against the edge of the table.

"Morrow?" After one last desperate wriggle, he returned his attention to Kate. "Are you related to John Morrow?"

"You *did* know Papa then!" Kate hoped this circumstance would serve to remind him that an advance would be most improper indeed. "Yes, I am John Morrow's daughter. Catherine." She extended her hand across the table, but Mr. Sinclair did not appear to notice.

"Catherine," he mused. "My own daughter's name is Catherine, but she is familiarly known as Kitty."

He had already stated—or repeatedly implied at least—that his daughter was called Kitty; and as Kate awkwardly withdrew her hand, she began to suspect that he was a trifle foxed. Her suspicion was confirmed when Mr. Barnes hurried back to the table with the promised glass of brandy, and Mr. Sinclair downed half of it in one great gulp and immediately ordered another. With a respectful bob of his head, the innkeeper once more trotted away.

"Yes, I was acquainted with your father," Mr. Sinclair said. "I didn't know him well, but I patronized his shop from time to time. Then, if I remember aright . . ." He took another deep sip of brandy in an apparent effort to refresh his memory. "If I remember aright, the shop closed and Mr. Morrow disappeared. I haven't seen him these ten years past."

"Twelve years," Kate corrected. "Papa closed the shop in St. George's a few weeks after Mama's death and opened a new one in Hamilton."

"He is to be commended for his foresight," Mr. Sinclair growled. "I wish I had guessed twelve years since that Hamilton would so shortly become the capital of the colony. I daresay your father has been amply rewarded for his cleverness."

No, he had not, Kate thought sadly. Papa had died before the capital was moved from St. George's to the young town of Hamilton, and she doubted he would have been "amply rewarded" by the transfer at any rate. Much as she'd adored her father, she had recognized early on that he had no head for business. But this was not the sort of information one volunteered to a stranger, and as she groped for an innocuous response, Mr. Barnes wheezed to a halt beside the table.

"I took the liberty of bringing you *two* brandies, sir," the landlord reported, setting a pair of identical, brimming glasses at Mr. Sinclair's elbow.

"Thank you, Barnes."

Mr. Sinclair drained his original glass, which was clearly not the first he had consumed that day, and the innkeeper plucked it up and galloped off again.

"Yes, I wish I had possessed your father's prescience." Mr. Sinclair punctuated his words with a generous sample of the fresh brandy. "*We*, I should have said; my partner was equally at fault." He glowered into his glass. "At this juncture, we can only hope there is truth in the maxim that it is better to act late than never. My partner has been in Hamilton for several months, establishing a branch of our business there."

Kate wondered which of his businesses he was referring to. Mr. Sinclair and his partner were engaged in shipbuilding and trading, but it was generally believed that privateering was by far their most profitable enterprise. Or piracy, depending on one's point of view. Papa had often remarked that the distinction was a vague one, and in Bermuda—where whole congregations had been known to leave church in the middle of the sermon so as to plunder a ship gone aground on the reefs—no one cared to know exactly where the legal line was drawn.

"Perhaps you have met my partner," Mr. Sinclair continued. "Samuel Wilcox?"

"No, I haven't met Mr. Wilcox."

"Well, I am sure your father knows him."

"I'm afraid not." Kate shook her head. "Papa died in the last fever epidemic."

"I am sorry to learn that, Miss Morrow. My wife was also taken by the fever, but that was many years ago. I collect you remained in Hamilton after your father's death? I should doubtlessly have encountered you before had you been in St. George's these last four years."

"I was not in Hamilton or St. George's either one," Kate replied. "I have been residing in Southampton with Mrs. Clement Todhunter."

"Todhunter." Mr. Sinclair shook his own head and swallowed another large portion of brandy. "Todhunter!" he repeated, his eyes widening in sudden comprehension. "Morrow! You are the . . . the . . ."

He stopped and choked down the rest of his brandy. Evidently he was not so jug-bitten as to have lost his senses altogether, Kate reflected dryly; he must have perceived that there was no delicate way to discuss Mrs. Todhunter's scandalous will. It was common knowledge in Bermuda that the irascible old widow had bequeathed the bulk of her estate to her paid companion, quite overlooking her grandniece in England. And—Mrs. Todhunter's solicitor had warned Kate—it was commonly supposed that Miss Morrow had taken shameless advantage of

her aged employer's diminished mental faculties
to enrich herself at the grandniece's expense. Mr.
Cottle lent no credence to such rumors, of course:
he knew as well as Kate that Mrs. Todhunter's
mind had remained razor-sharp till the very end.

But there was no delicate way to explain that
either and, Kate thought defensively, no need to
do so. She wasn't obliged to persuade Mr. Sinclair
that she had earned every farthing of her legacy
during the four interminable years she had served
as Mrs. Todhunter's abigail and secretary and
confidante.

"Yes," she rejoined instead. "Mrs. Todhunter
left me a very generous inheritance." She realized
even as the words emerged that Mr. Sinclair
would hardly regard five thousand pounds as
"very generous"; he and Mr. Wilcox could reap
that much profit in a month.

"I see."

Mr. Sinclair essayed a solemn nod and groped
for his second glass of brandy. He had behaved
astonishingly well thus far, but his head was now
wobbling on his neck, and his unsteady hand
nearly overturned the glass. Sooner or later, Kate
calculated, he *would* take leave of his senses; and
she peered nervously over her shoulder, praying
that Mr. Barnes would shortly deliver her meal.

"And when you received this generous
inheritance"—Mr. Sinclair spoke in the slow,
careful syllables of a drunk—"you decided to
resettle in St. George's."

"No." There was no sign of Mr. Barnes, and
Kate looked reluctantly back at Mr. Sinclair.
"When I received my legacy from Mrs. Todhunter,
I decided to settle in England. I booked passage on
the *Queen Anne*—"

"What a delightful coincidence!" he interposed. "I am to sail on the *Queen Anne* as well.

If she ever sails." His face fell, and he scowled into his glass again. "I closed my house on Tuesday, and I've been staying with friends since then, but I felt I could impose on them no longer. So I shall also be trapped at the Palmetto until the weather improves. Let us hope that will be soon, Miss Morrow."

He raised his glass as if to toast this hope, and at that moment, to Kate's relief, Mr. Barnes loomed up beside the table and set a steaming plate in front of her.

"Perhaps you would like some dinner, Mr. Sinclair?" she suggested. She was given to understand that food tended to mitigate the effect of strong spirits.

"No, thank you. Just bring another glass of brandy if you please, Barnes."

"Yes, sir."

The landlord sped away, and Mr. Sinclair—apparently reassured that his provisions would shortly be replenished—downed half the contents of the glass in his hand.

"So we shall be together on the *Queen Anne*," he reiterated. Lacking a napkin, he wiped his mouth on the sleeve of his tailcoat. "Do you have relatives in England, Miss Morrow?"

"Yes, Mama was the niece of a baronet in Cumberland."

"And your granduncle is still living?" Mr. Sinclair frowned. "He must be quite elderly."

"No," Kate admitted. "Mama's uncle died shortly after she and Papa emigrated to Bermuda, and the title passed to a distant cousin. Mama had no contact with him—the cousin, that is—but I hope . . ."

She lapsed into silence. Though she had not formulated a specific plan, she had hoped to present herself to her titled relative and prevail on him to introduce her into society. But she had never voiced this notion aloud, and she belatedly realized how foolish it would sound to an objective listener. Sir Randolph Edgerton had been dead for almost forty years; Kate knew of his existence only because his was one of the portraits she had so avidly studied during her childhood. It was entirely possible that the title had died by now as well, destroying her one tenuous connection to the British peerage. And even if the title survived, was there any reason to suppose that the current baronet would consent to take a strange cousin-much-removed under his wing? To the contrary, he would probably be horrified to learn that a young woman of two-and-twenty—related, however distantly, to him—had ventured thousands of miles across the sea without a chaperon.

Kate's stomach churned again, and her appetite, which had been none too hearty to begin with, vanished altogether. "I hope to locate Mama's family," she concluded lamely, no longer certain this was true.

"I have the advantage of you in that reshpect," Mr. Sinclair said. He was still speaking very slowly, but his words had begun to slur. "My father was the second son of a viscount, and though my grandfather and uncles are deceased, I have continued to correshpond with my cousin. Cousin Horace is the present Viscount Latimer."

"Umm," Kate muttered.

She feared he was at the point of relating the whole history of the Sinclair family, and she cast about for a courteous avenue of escape. In normal circumstances, she would remain at table until Mr. Sinclair had finished his meal, but it was growing increasingly evident that he did not intend to eat. Yes, abundantly evident: Mr. Barnes brought another glass of brandy to the table, and after draining the glass in his hand, Mr. Sinclair mumbled his order for yet another.

"I shall be residing with Cousin Horace in London," he went on as the innkeeper once more bustled away. "His town house is situated in Charles Street. Number one, to be exact; just where Charles Street intersects with Berkeley Square."

"Umm," Kate grunted again.

She dropped her eyes to the table and conceived an idea. Perhaps, if she cut her fish into tiny pieces and distributed the pieces artfully round her plate, she could claim that she had finished her own meal and beg to be excused. She picked up her fork.

"Do you plan to be in England long?" she asked, seeking to distract Mr. Sinclair's attention from her delicate surgical endeavor.

"I did not *plan* to go to England in the first place," he snapped. "My plan was . . ."

He sputtered to a halt, and Kate detected the click of his glass against his teeth.

"I found myself with an unpleasant duty to perform," he resumed. "I could have handled it by letter, but as I had never visited England, I decided to travel there in person."

His reference to an "unpleasant duty" piqued Kate's curiosity, but she judged it best not to pursue the matter. She kept her eyes on her plate and continued to dissect her grouper.

"Did I mention that my parents actually intended to settle in Virginia?" Mr. Sinclair said.

"Er . . . no." Kate had succeeded in separating the fish into several dozen segments, and she discreetly began to push them toward the edges of the plate.

"Yes. When Papa and Mama set out from

Plymouth, they intended to go to America, but their ship stopped at St. George's to unload and take on cargo. They were so enchanted with Bermuda that they elected to stay."

It was not an unusual story, Kate reflected: many Englishmen had immigrated to the island more or less by accident. Indeed, the very first British settlers had been bound for Virginia when a hurricane wrecked their vessel on the uninhabited shores of Bermuda. Her father's arrival, though not nearly so dramatic, had been equally fortuitous. Papa's regiment had been dispatched to Bermuda during the American rebellion, and like Mr. Sinclair's parents, he had fallen in love with the beautiful scenery and mild climate and chosen to stay. He had returned to England only long enough to resign his commission and marry his childhood sweetheart—

"Papa often commented how lucky it was that their journey was interrupted." Mr. Sinclair might have been reading Kate's mind. "Had he settled in Virginia, he would doubtlessly have become a planter, and I should be struggling to make my way in a new nation. As it is, two generations of Sinclairs have grown wealthy by seizing American ships in times of war."

And the ships of numerous other countries, Kate thought wryly. Fortunately for the men in Mr. Sinclair's profession, England was almost always at war with someone.

"But now the Americans have taken their revenge," he said grimly.

Kate bit back a giggle. Apparently Mr. Sinclair viewed the recent peace treaty between the United States and Britain as a personal affront—a devious American plot solely designed to deprive him and Mr. Wilcox of their major source of

income. Hardly a surprising attitude; she had
observed that all men, even gentle Papa, were
impossibly egotistic. She studied her plate and
decided that she had arranged the grouper too
neatly: there was a perfect circle round the rim
and nothing in the middle.

"Revenge?" she repeated aloud, raking a few
morsels of fish back toward the center of the
plate. "What sort of revenge, Mr. Sinclair?"

"They have stolen my daughter," he hissed.

"Stolen!" Kate's eyes flew up, and her jaws
sagged with shock. "The Americans *abducted*
Kitty?"

"No, but they might as well have done so." Mr.
Sinclair glared fuzzily over the rim of his glass.
"She eloped with an American merchant. A brazen
young man; he had the gall to call on me and offer
for Kitty's hand. Offer! Ha!"

He drained his glass and smashed it furiously on
the table. "What did he have to offer, Miss
Morrow?" he demanded rhetorically. "He's a
fellow of no breeding whatever with a pathetic
little business in Richmond. I refused him, of
course, and Kitty pretended to accept my
decision. And then, the very day she turned
twenty-one, she packed her things, left me a note,
and sailed off to Virginia with him. That was three
weeks ago, and if they aren't wed yet, they will be
shortly."

He stared gloomily into his empty glass, and
Kate felt a prickle of alarm. She had noticed at the
outset that Mr. Sinclair was flushed, but his color
had now darkened to a most unhealthy shade of
crimson.

"Do not tease yourself about it," she said
soothingly. "Kitty would have been hard-pressed
to find a husband in Bermuda."

The sea was a harsh mistress, exacting an

appalling payment in lives before she grudgingly surrendered her treasures. It had once been estimated that the perils of seafaring took such a toll of the island's male population that women outnumbered men by three to one, and though Kate judged this figure a trifle exaggerated, she had perceived long since that there was a dire shortage of eligible bachelors. It was one of the many reasons she had determined to remove to England.

"Kitty would not have been required to find a husband in Bermuda!" Mr. Sinclair roared. "I was well in the way of wedding her to an earl! Well, the heir to an earl," he amended, his voice dropping to a mere shout. "The son of Lord Halstead. His lordship was highly agreeable to the match, but did Kitty appreciate my efforts? No!"

He slammed his fist on the table, and his glass tipped over and rolled toward the edge. By a great stroke of luck, Mr. Barnes was just arriving with Mr. Sinclair's latest order, and the innkeeper nimbly rescued the wayward glass before it could tumble to the floor.

"Is something amiss with the service, sir?" he inquired anxiously.

"No, the service is shplendid. Pray bring me another brandy, Barnes."

The landlord bowed away, and Kate examined Mr. Sinclair with growing concern. His face had turned from crimson to purple, rivulets of perspiration trickled down his fleshy cheeks, and he could barely fasten his trembling fingers around the stem of his glass. At length, however, he managed to guide the glass to his mouth, and the fresh infusion of spirits seemed to calm him a bit.

"I am sure you would not have been so ungrateful, Miss Morrow," he said with a heavy sigh. "As ungrateful as my wretched daughter, I mean. No, I daresay you would have been thrilled if your father had arranged to introduce you to the son of an earl."

Kate's fascination with Mr. Sinclair's problems had briefly led her to forget her own, and his words jolted her back to reality. He had pointed out the "delightful" coincidence that they were to sail together on the *Queen Anne*, but apart from that, they had absolutely nothing in common. Mr. Sinclair was a rich, powerful man, closely connected to a viscount and friendly with at least one earl. Catherine Morrow had a scant five thousand pounds to her name and knew not a single person in England . . .

The panic began to gnaw at her stomach again, and she returned her attention to her plate. It needed a little more work, she saw; the upper right quadrant was suspiciously bare.

"And that is preshishely what I shall do," Mr. Sinclair continued triumphantly. "When we reach London, I shall present you to Lord Halstead's son. And Lord Halstead himself, of course, and my coushin Viscount Latimer. You will enjoy all the benefits Kitty disdained, and we shall leave her to rot in Virginia."

Kate's fork slipped through her fingers, and her eyes darted back across the table. He was speaking as a wounded father, she cautioned herself, and he was very foxed indeed. But she could not quell a flood of optimism. Maybe Mr. Sinclair was another miracle: her entrée to the lofty pinnacle of British society.

"I should welcome any assistance you might be kind enough to provide," she said carefully.

"We shall dishcush it on the ship." Mr. Sinclair sketched a paternal smile, then peered blearily out the window. "And I believe we shall sail tomorrow. The rain has nearly ended."

Yes, it had, Kate saw, following his gaze, and she glimpsed a hint of sunset behind the clouds. She doubted she would be granted a better opportunity to excuse herself, and she pushed her plate away.

"I fancy you are right," she said. "And if we are to depart tomorrow, we should both get an adequate night's rest."

"Go along, Miss Morrow." He vaguely fluttered his free hand. "I shall have another brandy or two and see you in the morning."

Kate nodded, rose, and hurried out of the dining room. She counted it quite likely that Mr. Sinclair would forget their conversation by morning, but there would be ample time during the voyage to remind him of his promises. She sped across the lobby and up the staircase, her feet—and her heart —lighter than they had been in years.

2

Kate's eyes flew open, and she bolted upright in the bed.

"Come in," she called.

She looked expectantly at the door, but there was no response, and she remembered that she was not in Mrs. Todhunter's Southampton mansion. Mr. Barnes's employees did not bring the morning water until the guest rang for service, and Kate wondered what had wakened her. Perhaps something had fallen to the floor. She gazed around her little room, but everything appeared to be in order. Her comb and brush and pot of rouge still sat atop the dressing table, bathed in a shaft of sunlight . . .

Sunlight! Kate leapt out of the bed, raced to the window, and yanked the curtains apart. The sky was a perfect, cloudless blue; were it not for the drooping fronds of the palms, the puddles in the square, one would never guess there had been a storm. Barring some damage to the vessel itself, the *Queen Anne* would definitely sail today.

Kate dropped the curtains and sped to her trunk. She had intended to wear her old "companion" clothes during the voyage, saving her new wardrobe till she reached England, but that was before she'd encountered Mr. Sinclair. He had undoubtedly been too foxed to notice her shabby attire last night, but this morning—or so Kate hoped—he would be sober. It was imperative to make a favorable impression on him—to persuade him that she was a young woman of considerable means and impeccable background worthy of his aid.

Kate opened the trunk, removed the topmost garment, and laid it on the bed. Miss Pryor, the mantua-maker in Hamilton, had described it as a "carriage dress," but Kate fancied it would do equally well for a journey by sea. She was too impatient to wait for hot water, and she poured the dregs of yesterday's water from the pitcher into the basin, stripped off her nightgown, splashed her face and body, donned a fresh set of underthings, and stepped into the dress. She hurried to the tiny mirror above the dressing table and anxiously studied her reflection as she fumbled with the hooks and eyes.

Kate had never cared for black; in her opinion, it inevitably suggested mourning. But Miss Pryor had advised her that black bombazine was the preferred fabric for a traveling costume, and Kate was compelled to admit that the gown was a handsome one—elegantly plain except for the double row of black crepe around the bottom of the skirt. She fastened the last hook, combed her hair, rubbed a bit of rouge on either cheek, and critically examined the final result. Yes, she decided, she projected just the right image: that of a prosperous, well-bred young lady seeking better opportunities abroad.

Kate dashed to the wardrobe, ripped her old dresses off the hangers, and shoved the dresses into her trunk. Apart from her cosmetic articles, she had not unpacked her valise, and she scooped up the items on the dressing table and tossed them in the smaller bag. And that was it, she saw, glancing round the room again. She had left several boxes with Mr. Cottle—boxes of books and portraits and mementos to be forwarded when she was settled in England—but everything else she owned was in her cases. She closed and fastened the lids, snatched her bonnet, gloves, and reticule from the wardrobe shelf, and rushed out of her room and down the staircase.

"Miss Morrow!" Mr. Barnes bounded out from behind the desk and galloped across the lobby to meet her. "Thank God you are awake!" His face was ashen, and he was wringing his hands in an agony of despair. "I have the most dreadful news."

Kate's shoulders sagged. Evidently the *Queen Anne* had sailed without her, and she had no one but herself to blame. When she'd realized the weather was improving, she should have instructed Mr. Barnes to knock her up at dawn.

"It's Mr. Sinclair," the landlord continued in a dramatic whisper. "He is dead."

"Dead?" Kate gasped. "Mr. Sinclair is *dead*? When . . . when. . . ?" Her head began to swim, and she sputtered to a halt.

"He left the dining room about midnight," Mr. Barnes responded, still in a whisper. "The moon was out by then, and he was confident the *Queen Anne* would sail this morning, so he instructed me to wake him at six. I sent Maggie to his room— Maggie is the senior chambermaid—and when he didn't answer the door, she opened it. And found Mr. Sinclair . . ."

He stopped and moved one hand in a long, straight line. It was an appallingly descriptive gesture: Kate could almost see Mr. Sinclair's corpse stretched upon his bed.

"But how?" she choked. "He seemed quite well last night . . ."

No, he had not seemed well at all, she remembered, her voice once more trailing off. She recalled his increasingly unhealthy color, his profuse perspiration, his trembling hands. Papa had subscribed to a theory that fat men were more subject than the average to sudden, fatal attacks, and Mr. Sinclair's abrupt demise tended to support this view. Apparently he had been so distressed by Kitty's elopement that he'd suffered some sort of seizure.

"You must find a way to notify his daughter," she resumed aloud.

"Yes." The innkeeper nodded. "I was in hopes you would consent to assist me in the performance of that sad duty. I daresay Miss Sinclair wouldn't feel the news so hard if you were present. You and she are nearly of an age, and you lost your own father not long ago. It will take but a few minutes; their house is just off the square—"

"But Miss Sinclair isn't there," Kate interposed. "Mr. Sinclair mentioned last evening that she recently left for Virginia."

"Virginia!" Mr. Barnes's eyes widened with horror. "It is a two-week voyage to Virginia. Two weeks there and two weeks back. I couldn't possibly keep the . . . ah . . ."

He moved his hand again, and Kate shuddered.

"Then I suggest you notify Mr. Wilcox of his partner's death," she said. "Next to Miss Sinclair, he is the logical person to make funeral arrangements."

"Mr. Wilcox is in Hamilton," the landlord wailed.

"True. But if you dispatch one of your servants with a message at once, he can be back by late tomorrow. In the interim, I fancy it would be safe to transfer the . . . er . . . remains to St. Peter's."

"You are right."

Mr. Barnes brightened a bit and bustled back toward the desk, beckoning Kate to follow. He reached below the counter, withdrew a sheet of paper and an envelope, and laid them on the surface.

"The pen is there," he said, indicating the inkstand beside the guest register. "Please stress to Mr. Wilcox that he must return to St. George's immediately."

"I?" Kate protested. "I must board the ship, Mr. Barnes."

"The *Queen Anne* isn't scheduled to sail for three quarters of an hour; I spoke with Captain Forbes when he left the inn. I shall order your luggage brought down while you write. Please, Miss Morrow." He pushed the paper toward her. "I am not very . . . very poetic."

Kate collected from this confession that, in fact, Mr. Barnes was barely literate—not an uncommon condition in Bermuda. She sighed and took the pen from the inkstand.

"March 30, 1816," she wrote in the upper right corner of the page.

Dear Mr. Wilcox,

I regret to inform you that your business partner, Mr. Robert Sinclair, expired at the Palmetto in St. George's sometime during the course of last night. Mr. Barnes, the landlord, intends to remove Mr. Sinclair's mortal remains to St. Peter's Church, but he is awaiting your advice in the matter of funeral arrangements. Mr. Barnes asked me to urge you to return to St. George's as soon as possible.

I further regret that I shall not be here to meet you personally, but I am departing for England within the hour. I trust you will communicate with Miss Sinclair in Richmond at the earliest opportunity.

Yours very truly,
Catherine Morrow

Kate blotted the letter, folded it, placed it in the envelope, and passed the envelope to Mr. Barnes. The innkeeper smiled his gratitude, but evidently he was not so grateful as to forgive her bill, which he now passed across the desk in turn. He had no difficulty with sums, Kate observed dryly: he had readily multiplied four nights times five shillings a night to produce a total of one pound. She pulled a one-pound note from her reticule, and Mr. Barnes deftly plucked it from her fingers and whisked it out of sight below the counter.

"Your bags are here," he announced, peering over her head. "My man will accompany you to the ship."

Kate felt a foolish prickle of tears behind her eyelids. Mr. Barnes and Papa had had a pleasant professional relationship—each had referred customers to the establishment of the other—but they had never been friends. And the innkeeper was certainly no friend of Kate's; she hadn't even thought of him during the dozen years since she had left St. George's. But his plump face was a Bermudian face, perhaps the last she would ever see, and she could not repress a sniffle.

"Hell and the devil," Mr. Barnes growled. He reached under the counter again and slapped her bank note back upon the top. "Here you are. Good luck to you, Miss Morrow."

She shook her head; she couldn't speak.

"I want you to keep it," he said gruffly. "It could be that this very pound will make your fortune in England. Get along with you now. There's no time to waste."

Nor was there. It was less than half a mile from the Palmetto to the docks—a ten-minute walk—but by the time Kate and Mr. Barnes's footman reached the *Queen Anne*, the ship was at the point of sailing. Captain Forbes stopped shouting orders long enough to nod her a curt welcome, after which he shrieked at one of his crew to bring her luggage aboard. This task had scarcely been accomplished when the captain bellowed for the plank to be lifted and the anchor raised, and the *Queen Anne* began to move.

No, the great ship didn't move, Kate soon amended: she fairly flew across the water. St. George's harbor receded with breathtaking speed, and the wind in Kate's face was so strong that she was hard put to keep her balance. Her leghorn hat blew off her head and tumbled to the nape of her neck, and—lest she lose the bonnet altogether—she untied the ribbons, took it off, and clutched it in her hand.

"Your cases have been removed to your cabin, Miss Morrow."

Kate started and spun around. Captain Forbes was standing beside her; she had not recognized his voice. Which, she surmised, was probably because she had not previously heard him speak in any tone below a roar.

"I'm sorry if I seemed a bit abrupt when you came aboard." The captain might have been reading her thoughts. "I was eager to get under way before the next storm arrived."

He waved vaguely into the distance, and Kate glanced over her shoulder. There was a bank of gray clouds on the western horizon, drifting slowly toward the now-hazy shore of Bermuda.

"That is all right," she murmured, turning back to Captain Forbes.

"I *hope* it is all right," he said grimly. "I am gambling that the storm will blow itself out before it catches us up. But we seamen are a superstitious lot, and I cannot but wonder if it was a mistake to sail this morning. In the circumstances."

"What . . . what circumstances?" Kate asked nervously.

"I was referring to Mr. Sinclair's death. I have never lost a passenger before. But Mr. Sinclair wasn't yet a passenger, was he?" Captain Forbes flashed a bright smile of relief, then sobered. "Forgive me, Miss Morrow. He may have been a close friend of yours."

"No." Kate shook her head. "No, I barely knew him."

But she realized even as she spoke that the brevity of their acquaintance didn't signify. She had come to count on Mr. Sinclair's assistance, and she had been so rushed since she learned of his death that she had had no chance to ponder the ramifications. Now they were all too clear. She would not be presented to earls and viscounts when she reached England; she would be entirely alone.

"Then let us pray for fair winds and good luck," Captain Forbes said jovially. "With a reasonable share of both, we should dock in Plymouth by the first of May. Now, if you will excuse me, I must check to be sure my men are steering us in the proper direction."

He bowed away, and Kate turned round again, but the coast of Bermuda had disappeared. There was nothing but empty sea behind her and only empty sea ahead. Much like her life, Kate thought, and she almost wished they would never get to England.

"Where to, miss?" The hackney driver hoisted Kate's valise to the rear-facing seat of the coach and peered up at her.

Where to indeed? she wondered dismally. She was so tired that she could scarcely hold her head erect, much less consider such a complicated question.

Unlike Captain Forbes, Kate was not particularly superstitious; though she had come to respect the power of fate in recent months, she regarded "fate" as a synonym for "chance." She did not believe in ghosts and similar phenomena, and—again unlike the captain—she did not suppose that Mr. Sinclair's restless spirit was in any way responsible for their arduous voyage. But there was no denying that their passage across the Atlantic had been unpleasant in the extreme.

To begin with, Captain Forbes had lost his gamble: the second storm had caught them up six-and-thirty hours out of St. George's and hounded the *Queen Anne* for nearly two weeks. Well, that wasn't quite accurate, Kate amended. The captain, with the aid of his seaman's instinct and sophisticated instruments, had identified three separate storms following one upon another in rapid succession, but Kate's untrained stomach failed to notice the lulls between them. According to her recollection, the ship had pitched and rolled unceasingly for eleven interminable days, and she was seasick every minute of every day.

Kate had never been especially religious either, but as the storm continued into the second week, she began to pray for an end to her misery. And—as so often seemed to happen—her prayers were answered rather more literally than she might have wished. She woke on the twelfth morning with the eerie sound of silence in her ears, and when she made her way up to the deck, she discovered another perfect day. The sky was clear, the ship was steady, there was no wind—

"No wind," Captain Forbes said, materializing at her side.

"Yes." Kate drew a deep, invigorating breath of air. "What a relief."

"Hardly a relief," he snapped. "We are all but becalmed. Another trick of Mr. Sinclair's, I'll warrant."

He went on to explain that seafaring men often described this windless condition as the "doldrums." Though doldrums generally occurred much nearer the equator, he added darkly, which was all the more reason to suspect that the late Mr. Sinclair had determined to punish them for sailing so quickly without him. Be that as it might, the *Queen Anne* was the finest ship afloat, and her sails would constantly be rerigged to take advantage of the slightest breeze. No other vessel could sail from Bermuda to England faster than the *Queen Anne*. Which was not to say, given the present unique and

distressing circumstances, that she would reach
Plymouth in her usual expeditious manner.

And she had not. On the first of May, their
estimated date of arrival, Captain Forbes glumly
calculated that they were little more than halfway
to Plymouth, and Kate began to fear that her careless wish would be granted and they would never
get to England. The next day, however (or the one
after that; Kate had lost all track of time), the wind
freshened, and the captain happily reported that,
at last, the ship was moving at maximum speed.
Kate derived scant comfort from this information:
when they had finally docked in Plymouth
yesterday, thirteen days late, she felt as if she had
spent several years aboard the *Queen Anne*.

Captain Forbes advised Kate to hire a post
chaise for the drive to London, but when she
learned that the cost of a private carriage was a
shilling a mile, she decided against such an
expensive means of transportation. Though Mr.
Cottle had supplied her with a letter of credit to
the Bank of England, she found it difficult to trust
in money she could neither see nor touch. She was
wholly confident only of the cash in her reticule,
and it had already been depleted by the payment
of her passage. She dared not waste eight precious
pounds on the journey from Plymouth to the
capital.

So she had set out in a stagecoach late the
previous afternoon, and this, she now owned, had
been a grievous error. She had been on the road
for twenty hours—jostled unmercifully about,
drifting briefly to sleep, immediately waking up
again—and she was physically and mentally
exhausted.

"Where to, miss?" the hackney driver
impatiently repeated.

Another mistake, Kate thought. Mr. Cottle had counseled her to lease a house in London before she left Bermuda; he was familiar with a number of realty agents who could execute a rental contract in her behalf. But she had wanted to select her own residence, and she hadn't realized until the stage reached the suburbs of the sprawling city how monumental the task would be. It would take days at the least, maybe weeks, and in the interim, she must have a place to stay.

"To . . . to an inn," she stammered weakly.

"Ye're *at* an inn." The driver emitted a snort of keen annoyance. "There ain't a better one in London."

He waved his hand, and Kate gazed over his head and studied the Bull and Mouth again. It was an enormous establishment and did appear to be well-kept, but she had sensed at once that it was not a proper domicile for a respectable young woman. The yard was as busy as the proverbial beehive, coaches racing in and out . . .

"I was hoping for something . . . something quieter," she said, returning her attention to the driver. "In a less busy part of town."

"A hotel, ye mean."

"Yes!" Kate had never seen a hotel, but she eagerly bobbed her head. "Yes, that's exactly what I mean. A hotel in a quiet area of the city."

"Well, that narrows the choice to two or three dozen places," the driver said sarcastically. "Could ye give me just a tiny hint what area of the city ye'd prefer?"

Kate clenched her hands, wishing for perhaps the thousandth time that Mr. Sinclair hadn't died. If he had sailed with her on the *Queen Anne*, they would undoubtedly have traveled on to London together. Mr. Sinclair, not needing to count his pennies, would have engaged a chaise, and the chaise would have whisked them directly to his cousin's home. After a warm welcome—a cup of tea, possibly dinner—Viscount Latimer would have recommended a suitable hotel . . .

Viscount Latimer. Tired as she was, Kate conceived the glimmer of an idea. It would be entirely proper for her to call on Lord Latimer and notify him of his cousin's death. Indeed, it was almost her *duty* to do so: the irresponsible Kitty might not think to write her father's relatives for months. If ever. His lordship would appreciate Kate's consideration and would surely help her locate appropriate lodgings. In fact, he might be so grateful that he would offer to let her reside with him until she found a house of her own. Might take it upon himself to introduce her into society . . .

"Number one Charles Street," she blurted out, remembering the direction Mr. Sinclair had mentioned.

"Ain't no hotel in Charles Street, miss."

"No, but I have . . . have friends there."

The driver nodded—albeit dubiously—closed the carriage door, mounted the box, and the coach clattered out of the innyard and into the street.

Kate had fancied that the rocking of the carriage would soon put her to sleep again, but the sights around her were so fascinating that, instead, she experienced a burst of nervous energy. They had hardly got under way when they passed a structure she recognized from pictures as St. Paul's Cathedral, and her lips parted with awe. Although, she reflected, the pictures were somewhat misleading. The drawings she had seen created the impression that the great church stood alone, its dome soaring toward the sky in solitary splendor; and in truth, it was surrounded by other buildings on every side. The neighborhood was clearly a commercial one—the footpaths thronged with bustling pedestrians—and she surmised, from an abundance of figures in black robes and white wigs, that Old Bailey was nearby.

And the traffic! Horses were a luxury in Bermuda, taxed at two pounds per year, and carriages were consequently reserved for the very rich. Mrs. Todhunter, prosperous as she was, had possessed only a small, battered buggy, drawn by a single horse, and even this modest equipage had been sufficient to attract respectful attention on the rare occasions Kate drove it into town. But the buggy would get no attention here; to the contrary, it would probably be trampled over within the first five minutes. There was a seemingly endless line of vehicles ahead of them, another streaming toward them—all fearfully close together and moving with alarming speed. An oncoming carriage turned in front of the hackney, clearing the horses' noses by mere inches, and as the driver shrieked a colorful assortment of curses, Kate hastily shifted her eyes back to the passing buildings.

Kate had no notion where Charles Street was, but at length, the changing scenery indicated that they were approaching a more residential section of the city. The great public buildings gave way to cozy shops, and the shops soon became interspersed with houses. The coach had made several confusing turns by now, and when it turned again, they entered a street entirely bordered by homes. The carriage careened around another corner, then halted so abruptly that Kate was nearly tumbled off the seat. She was still catching her breath when the driver threw the door open.

"We're here," he announced gratuitously. "Number one Charles Street."

Kate peered at the house and could not quell a stab of disappointment. There was nothing to distinguish Viscount Latimer's residence from the neighboring homes; like the rest, it was tall and narrow and seemed pathetically small in comparison to Mrs. Todhunter's mansion. Indeed, Lord Latimer's house was among the plainest in the street: no columns adorned the facade, and the windows lacked any decoration beyond the painted sashes.

More to the point, Kate could detect no sign of activity, and she belatedly perceived the flaw in her plan. Though Mr. Sinclair had obviously expected his cousin to be in London when he arrived, it was entirely possible that Lord Latimer was out for the afternoon. If such was the case, his lordship's butler would desire Kate to leave a message; he would not invite her to hang about until the viscount returned. And—a further flaw— if Lord Latimer was home, there was no assurance he would greet her with the fervent appreciation she had envisioned. He had never even met his Bermudian cousin. He might well thank Kate politely for her information and send her on her way without so much as a drop of tea.

The driver reached for her valise, and she pushed his hand aside.

"Not just yet," she said. "I daresay I should speak with my . . . ah . . . friends before you unload the baggage. Could you wait a moment?"

"Of course, miss."

He assisted her out of the coach, and Kate glanced despairingly down at the skirt of her carriage dress. She had replaced the dress in her trunk after the first night at sea and not put it on again till Captain Forbes sighted the coast of England, but her long hours in the stage had reduced it to a shapeless mass of wrinkles. She smoothed the creases as best she could and retied the ribbons of her bonnet.

"Ye do understand," the driver added, "that every minute of me waiting time will cost ye."

Kate had not understood this, and she ground her teeth with frustration. Her initial inclination was to instruct him to wait regardless of the fee, but she did not know how long she might be inside the house. It would be the height of foolishness to spend her limited resources on a hackney coach sitting idly in the street.

"Then you may unload my luggage immediately," she snapped.

This, it soon proved, was a wise decision, for after the driver had carried her valise to the doorstep, untied her trunk from the roof of the carriage, and deposited the trunk beside the valise, he demanded half a pound as his fare.

"Half a pound!" Kate protested. "We couldn't have come more than two miles! I was told that the normal charge is a shilling a mile."

"The normal charge for a chaise." The driver sketched a frosty, largely toothless smile. "They don't have no traffic to contend with."

"But . . ."

But it would probably be futile to argue any further. No, worse than futile; it would be *horrifying* if Viscount Latimer observed her quarreling with a lowly hackney driver. Kate opened her reticule, extracted two five-shilling coins, and laid them in the driver's outstretched palm. She had surrendered much too quickly, she collected, because he pocketed the coins at once, making no attempt to wheedle a tip. He launched into a cheerful, tuneless whistle, danced merrily down the steps, fairly leapt to the box of the carriage, and reined his horses round. The coach rattled away, and she fancied she could still hear him whistling as it turned the first corner and trotted out of sight.

Kate looked back at the house and realized, again too late, that she should have requested the driver to set her cases on the side of the doorstep. As it was, they were situated squarely in front of the door, and it appeared she had taken it for granted that Lord Latimer would ask her to stay. She moved the valise against the iron railing at her right, but she couldn't manage the trunk alone, and with a sigh and a final nervous tug at her hat, she rang the bell.

"Yes?" The butler (or so Kate presumed) gazed impassively down at her.

"Good afternoon," she gulped. "I am Catherine—"

"Catherine?"

A woman loomed up behind the butler, then elbowed her way impatiently past him, sailed across the threshold, and spread her arms.

"Kitty!" She took another forward step and clasped Kate in a warm, welcoming embrace. "Kitty, my dear child! How delighted I am that you are here at last!"

3

The use of her old nickname, the gentle arms around her, the scent of a light perfume spun Kate dizzily into the past. It might almost be her mother holding her, and when the woman released her and stood away, Kate saw that, in fact, she looked rather like Mama. No, Kate amended, she looked as Mama would have had she lived: she was perhaps five-and-fifty years of age, with pale blue eyes and blond hair liberally streaked with gray. But this wasn't Mama; it must be Lady Latimer. And she had obviously mistaken Kate for Mr. Sinclair's daughter.

"Lady Latimer," she said. "I am—"

"Let us not stand on ceremony, dear," her ladyship interposed. "I wish you to call me Cousin Jane, and I hope you will permit me to call you Kitty."

"Kate," she instinctively corrected.

"Kate?" Lady Latimer frowned. "I was sure your father referred to you as Kitty."

"He did when I was younger, he and Mama both, but later . . ." She realized that she was merely reinforcing her ladyship's misapprehension, and she shook her head to clear it. "But that is beside the point. I am not—"

"I understand." Lady Latimer patted Kate's sleeve. "You are not a child any longer, and you don't want to be called by your childhood name. I had a similar problem. I was known as Janie when I was small, and my papa continued to use that name from time to time till the day he died. How I hated it! Rest assured that I shall call you Kate."

"No, you *don't* understand," Kate protested. "I should have explained at once that—"

"No explanations are required," her ladyship interrupted soothingly. "Cousin Robert stated that you would arrive at the beginning of May, but I am well aware that ocean voyages are subject to unavoidable delay. The Season is barely under way, and you have missed very little. Fortunately, I anticipated you might be late and scheduled my own ball for the first of June."

"I am certain your ball will be lovely," Kate said. "But I am—"

"My poor dear! Of course you are too tired to think about an assembly! Indeed, you must be exhausted. How thoughtless of me to keep you standing on the doorstep."

Lady Latimer seized Kate's hand and tugged her across the threshold. "Pray see to Miss Sinclair's luggage, Adams," she instructed the butler. "Have the footboys take her bags to the rose bedchamber. And then bring a tea tray to the saloon."

"No!" Kate insisted. "I—"

"My poor dear," her ladyship repeated. "I daresay you are too tired even to climb the stairs. We shall have our tea in the library. Bring the tray to the library, Adams. Come along, Kate."

The latter command was quite gratuitous, for Lady Latimer was still clutching Kate's hand. She strode across the vestibule, fairly dragging Kate beside her, and opened the door on the left side. The library was far smaller than Mrs. Todhunter's, Kate observed, and rather the worse for wear; but, perhaps for these very reasons, she found it vastly more inviting. Mrs. Todhunter's cavernous library had resembled a museum: one hesitated to remove a book from the immaculate shelves, much less sprawl on one of the elegant couches or curl up in one of the chairs. Viscount Latimer's books were arranged helter-skelter in their cases—suggesting that they were regularly, lovingly read—and the Adam furniture was sagging from years of use.

"The library is very pleasant," Kate remarked aloud.

"I'm glad you think so. Please feel free to borrow any books you like. The house is yours. Well, not *literally* yours, of course . . ."

Lady Latimer's voice trailed off, and she abruptly dropped Kate's hand. "Oh, dear." She sighed. "I didn't intend to bring up such delicate matters immediately after your arrival, but maybe it's for the best. Maybe it wasn't made clear that the town house is not part of the entailed property."

"Entailed property," Kate echoed. She knew the meaning of the term, but it made no sense in the context of the conversation.

"Yes. That is to say that the town house isn't included in your father's inheritance."

"Inheritance?" Kate knit her brows in puzzlement.

"You didn't know?" Lady Latimer gasped. "You did not receive Mr. Vincent's letter?"

"Mr. Vincent?" Kate was beginning to entertain the impression that her ladyship had lapsed into a foreign tongue.

"Horace's solicitor. He wrote Cousin Robert above a year ago to advise him—advise Cousin Robert, that is—that Horace had died."

"Lord Latimer is dead?" Kate tottered a step or two and sank upon the striped mahogany sofa.

"*Horace* is dead. Which means, of course, that your father is now Viscount Latimer." Her ladyship paused, ruefully shaking her own head. "I should have surmised that Mr. Vincent's communication went astray. Cousin Robert's last letter was directed to Horace, but I fancied his secretary had made an error. As you are undoubtedly aware, your father's secretary addresses and posts his correspondence. But the message itself was in Cousin Robert's hand, and it contained no mention of Horace's death. It said only that you would reach London early in May."

She stopped again and heaved another sigh. "Yes, I should have perceived that your father didn't know

Horace was . . . was gone. At the least, he would have extended his condolences. Indeed, I daresay that had he known, he would have elected to accompany you to England."

She must speak now, Kate thought. If she waited an instant longer, her deception—however innocent at the outset—would become a deliberate masquerade. There was still time, barely time, to resolve the confusion with her integrity intact. She could stand up, claim that exhaustion had temporarily clouded her mind, identify herself . . .

But what if she did not? the seductive voice of temptation whispered. Though Kate was, in truth, too exhausted to puzzle out the precise chronology of the Sinclair family drama, the general outline of the plot was clear. Viscount Latimer had died, leaving Mr. Sinclair his title and some share of his estate. Mr. Sinclair, ignorant of this legacy, had arranged to send his daughter to England, where his British cousins were prepared to give her a glittering come-out. But Kitty had defied him; a few weeks before her scheduled departure, she had eloped to Virginia, and Mr. Sinclair had decided to sail in her stead. He had alluded to an "unpleasant duty," Kate remembered, and she now guessed he'd been referring to his impending moment of reckoning. The humiliating moment when he would be compelled to inform Lord and Lady Latimer that his daughter had disdained their kindness and run away with an impecunious American merchant. In fact, he had used that very word: he had pledged that Kate would enjoy all the benefits Kitty had *disdained.*

And why shouldn't she? The tantalizing voice in Kate's head whispered relentlessly on. Lady Latimer believed her to be Kitty Sinclair, and who was to set her straight? Mr. Sinclair was dead. Viscount

Latimer was dead as well; there would be no awkward questions about the letters he and his cousin had exchanged. That left only Kitty herself, and Kate had already concluded that she was unlikely to write her English relatives in the near future. Indeed, Kitty might not learn of her father's death for months to come. Kate had mentioned in her message to Mr. Wilcox that Miss Sinclair was in Richmond, but Kitty was no longer "Miss Sinclair." Kate didn't know her married name, and she doubted Mr. Wilcox did either: Mr. Sinclair would not have told his business partner of his daughter's unsuitable *parti*. It would be hard enough for Mr. Wilcox to locate Kitty without a specific direction; without a surname, it would be all but impossible.

So there was no reason to hesitate, the voice assured Kate. No one would discover her impersonation, and no one would suffer any harm if she pretended to be Kitty. She certainly didn't intend to steal anything. Not even room and board: she would proceed with her plan to lease a house. Though she probably wouldn't have to keep the house for long. Many eligible young peers would be eager to court the daughter of a viscount—

"How very ironic." Lady Latimer shattered Kate's reverie. "Had Horace died a few days earlier, the present bumblebath could have been avoided. Not that I wish he *had* died earlier," she added hastily. "But if he had, Daniel could have told your father of his death. As it was, Daniel was already en route to Bermuda."

"Daniel," Kate repeated carefully.

"Lord Halstead."

The earl, Kate recollected. The earl who had been "highly agreeable" to a match between his son and Kitty Sinclair.

"He was immensely taken with you, dear," her ladyship continued. "Quite disappointed that Cousin Robert would not allow you to return to England with him. But as you know, your father judged it best to keep you in Bermuda till you were of legal age."

A decision Mr. Sinclair must have come to regret most bitterly, Kate reflected; had he sent Kitty abroad when he had the chance, she would never have met her "brazen" American suitor. But that was neither here nor there. The voice of temptation had reckoned without Lord Halstead, and Kate realized—with a peculiar blend of regret and relief—that he posed an insurmountable obstacle to her charade. The earl had met the real Kitty Sinclair—

"I'm afraid I have tragic news in that regard as well." Lady Latimer sat beside Kate and once more took her hand. "Daniel, too, has . . . has departed. He died very suddenly the first Sunday in March. I am certain of the date because we were engaged to attend church together. As we often did. You can imagine my shock when one of his servants arrived in Daniel's stead and informed me he had collapsed while dressing. I had seen him just the night before, and he appeared to be in splendid health."

The circumstances were so similar to those of Mr. Sinclair's death that Kate could not repress a shiver. It seemed that fate was determined to have its way, to grant her no escape.

"I am sorry to have been so abrupt." Lady Latimer had obviously misinterpreted Kate's tremor. "I wrote to your father the week following Daniel's death, but I realized my letter wouldn't reach Bermuda before your departure. Perhaps you'll be comforted to learn that Gilbert has adjusted admirably to his loss."

Kate collected that Gilbert was Lord Halstead's son.

"I am of the opinion that it is imperative to keep busy after the death of a loved one," her ladyship went on. "I have had to manufacture activities— embroidery, long walks, gardening when I'm in the country. But I believe Gilbert is sufficiently busy with the management of his estate. Yes, I daresay he's discovering that it is no easy matter to be an earl. Well, you will soon have the opportunity to ask him yourself. By a happy coincidence, he will be here for dinner this evening."

Coincidence? Kate thought wildly. No, it was another stroke of fate, and she began to tremble. Not merely a shiver this time: she fancied she could hear her bones rattling, and her heart was pounding a mad tattoo against her ribs.

"My dear child!" Lady Latimer dropped her hand and gazed at her with dismay. "You are shaking like a leaf! Where is Adams? He should have brought the tea long since."

She glanced at the library door, then looked back at Kate. "But maybe tea is not the thing for you just now. It does tend to jangle one's nerves, doesn't it? And your nerves are quite jangled enough already. Perhaps you should go directly to your bedchamber and have a nice long nap."

Kate dimly perceived that she had been granted one last chance to confess her true identity. Lady Latimer's transcendent virtue was that of kindness; she was not burdened with a surfeit of intelligence. Kate could agree that she was prodigious nervous indeed—so nervous and fatigued that she had inadvertently misrepresented herself. But the voice was hissing in her mind again, and she did not.

"Thank you, Cousin Jane," she murmured instead.

"I shall forgo the tea and proceed directly to my room."

"There." The maid fastened Mrs. Todhunter's pearls around Kate's neck and stepped away from the cheval glass. "Is everything satisfactory, Miss Sinclair?"

In fact, Kate thought, she looked far better than she had anticipated. She had fancied when she tumbled into bed that she could sleep the clock around, but a four-hour nap and a hot bath had proved remarkably restorative. The color had returned to her cheeks, and though there had been no time to wash her hair, Sally, the maid, had skillfully repaired it. No, more than repaired, Kate amended. She had worn her hair in the Roman style for some months, but she could never manage to position the bandeau just right or arrange the front curls properly round her face. Sally had accomplished both tasks to perfection, and the improvement was astonishing.

"Yes," Kate responded aloud. "Everything is quite satisfactory."

"Then if you will excuse me, I'll start pressing the rest of your clothes." Sally bounded to the bed, scooped up the wrinkled garments she had previously draped over the footboard, and scurried back across the carpet. "Don't forget," she added, fumbling with the doorknob, "that dinner will be served at seven."

It would be easy to grow accustomed to such luxury, Kate reflected as Sally retreated into the corridor. Not the luxury of her surroundings: the rose bedchamber was somewhat smaller than the room she'd occupied at Todhunter House, and its furnishings were no more elegant. But never before, in all her two-and-twenty years, had Kate had a personal servant. To the contrary, she had cooked and cleaned for Papa, and it had often fallen to her to assist Mrs. Todhunter's slaves in the performance of their duties. The slaves had been freed upon the old widow's death, and during the weeks Kate had remained at the mansion, she had been attended only by the ancient housekeeper. Who, to say the truth, required more service than she provided. It was quite delightful to have an abigail at one's beck and call—drawing one's bath and arranging one's hair and pressing one's clothes . . .

But she did not intend to take undue advantage of the situation, Kate sternly reminded herself. With Lady Latimer's assistance, she could probably locate a house by the end of the week, and she would request such assistance before the evening was over. The mantel clock began to chime the hour, and she hurried out of the bedchamber and down the staircase.

Kate heard a murmur of voices as she sped along the first-floor corridor and surmised that Gilbert had arrived. Should she call him "Gilbert"? she wondered. Though Mr. Sinclair and Lord Halstead had obviously hoped to promote a match between their children, the children themselves hadn't met. There was no assurance that Gilbert—now he was himself the Earl of Halstead—would care to undertake the courtship his late father had favored. No assurance that he would find Kate in the least attractive. Indeed, she might not find him attractive either.

Kate stopped at the landing and peered into the vestibule, but the man chatting with Lady Latimer was positioned with his back to the stairs. He appeared to be tall and lean, with broad shoulders, a narrow waist, and long, slender legs. But cleverly tailored clothes could hide a multitude of sins. It was entirely possible that Gilbert's brown tailcoat had been nipped in at the middle and his almond pantaloons designed to hang rather loosely.

"Here she is!" Her ladyship glanced up and flashed a radiant smile. "Are you feeling better, dear?"

The earl started to turn, and Kate—her face warming with embarrassment—dropped her eyes and proceeded down the steps. It belatedly occurred to her that Lady Latimer might be hoping to promote a union as well; she believed Kate to be a cousin, and the Halsteads were evidently close friends of the Sinclairs. If she judged Gilbert truly odious, she must take care not to betray her opinion. She reached the entry hall, looked up, and stumbled to a halt, her breath catching in her throat.

Lord Halstead wasn't unusually handsome, Kate realized even as she struggled to regain her composure. Not in the classic sense at least: his features were too irregular to fit any artistic conception of beauty. Like Kate herself, he had high, sharp cheekbones and hollow cheeks, but the similarity ended there. Gilbert's chin was square, as were his jaws, and his nose was disproportionately short. Short and slightly uptilted at the end, which lent him a mischievous, boyish aspect.

No, the earl's face was quite ordinary until one observed his eyes, and then everything else dwindled to insignificance. Literally dwindled—his eyes were excessively large, overpowering the rest of his features—but it was their color that rendered them so compelling. Though Kate was at a loss to decide exactly what color they were. Amber? They were certainly paler than brown, but she suspected that in some lights, some moods, they might grow paler yet. Might turn to the tawny gold of a cat's eyes . . .

She became aware that the eyes in question, whatever their hue, were reciprocating her scrutiny, and she hastily peered down again. Gilbert's clothes hid no sins after all, she saw: his stomach was flat both above and below the waistband of his pantaloons, and the latter were cut so snugly as to leave little to the imagination. Her breath had returned by now, but she could feel the pulses racing in her neck, leaping in her wrists. Far from being odious, Lord Halstead was the most attractive man she had ever encountered, and for the first time, she was unreservedly thankful that Lady Latimer had mistaken her for Kitty Sinclair.

"Here she is," her ladyship repeated. "I was just telling Cousin Jeffrey of your arrival, dear."

"Cousin . . . Jeffrey?" Kate's heart slowed to a dull thud, and she could not keep the disappointment from her voice.

"We needn't be so formal," he said. Apparently —fortunately—he had misinterpreted her tone. "Jeffrey will do very nicely. And I believe you are known as Kate?"

"Yes," she mumbled.

She shifted her gaze back to his face and noticed that his hair was several shades darker than his eyes: light brown shot all through with strands of gold. She wondered about the precise relationship between him and Lady Latimer. Her ladyship had called him "cousin," but he seemed too young to be a first cousin to the viscountess or her late husband either one. Too young by a full generation; he could not be much above thirty. So he must be a distant relative, Kate concluded, like the Edgerton cousin who had inherited her granduncle's estate.

More to the point, Kate wondered if Jeffrey was married. He was alone this evening, but there might well be a Cousin Anne or Cousin Elizabeth sequestered at one of his country estates, tending their numerous children—

"Jeffrey is in town for the Season." Lady Latimer interrupted Kate's dark speculation. "Staying here with me." She waved vaguely round the foyer, as if to suggest that Jeffrey's bed was located in one of the shadowy corners. "And I am in hopes that this is the year he will *finally* take a wife."

She patted Jeffrey's sleeve with fond exasperation, and Kate's heart speeded up again. Though she herself would not remain at Lady Latimer's for long, it was inevitable that she and Jeffrey would be thrown together during the upcoming Seasonal festivities.

The doorbell pealed, and Lady Latimer spun around and threw the door open.

"Gilbert!" She clapped her hands with delight. "I have the most wonderful surprise! Kate has arrived at last."

She stepped aside, and another young man loomed up behind her, blinking a bit in the dim light of the vestibule.

"Here she is," her ladyship said once more. "Our dear cousin, Kate Sinclair. Your fiancé."

4

Fiancée! Kate's polite smile of greeting froze on her mouth, and her eyes widened with horror. Dear God! She had never dreamed . . .

But she should have, she chided herself, for it was abundantly clear in retrospect that Mr. Sinclair and the late Lord Halstead had reached some sort of nuptial agreement. Mr. Sinclair had not said that he was "attempting" to wed Kitty to the son of an earl or "hoping" to arrange a match; he had stated that he was "well in the way" of doing so. In fact, Kate now recalled, Lord Halstead had wished to escort Kitty to England— a most peculiar desire if she were merely the daughter of a casual colonial acquaintance. And while it would certainly have been "unpleasant" for Mr. Sinclair to inform his British cousins that Kitty had defied him, it would hardly have been a "duty." No, the duty was the painful one of advising Lord Halstead that Kitty had abrogated the agreement and eloped with another man. As it was, Gilbert believed he and Kate were engaged—

"Kate?" The earl was still blinking, and when he looked down, his eyes didn't quite meet hers. "I was under the impression that you are called Kitty."

"She *was* called Kitty," Lady Latimer said. "You know how stubborn fathers can be . . ."

She chattered on, and Kate took the opportunity to study the new Lord Halstead. He and Jeffrey were approximately the same age, she estimated, but they shared no other characteristic. She supposed that by any traditional standard, Gilbert would be judged the handsomer: his face was pleasantly rounded, and he had a long, straight, aristocratic nose. But something was missing, and at length, Kate perceived that Gilbert had no color. He would make a splendid statue, but in a painting, his pale skin and gray eyes and sandy hair would run together.

"At any rate," Lady Latimer concluded, "she would prefer to be called Kate."

"Then Kate it is," Gilbert agreed. "And if I may say so," he added gallantly, "you are quite as lovely as Papa promised. Although . . ." His eyes had adjusted to the light by now, and he frowned. "I expected you to be taller. Papa told me you were very tall."

What constituted very tall? Kate wondered. She was nearly five and a half feet in height, which was well above the average for a woman.

"But Daniel was exceedingly short," her ladyship said. "He thought *everyone* was tall."

"That is true." Gilbert laughed. "He never could puzzle out why I grew so large."

Kate discreetly glanced from him to Jeffrey and back again. Much as he might wish to believe otherwise, Gilbert wasn't notably tall—he stood midway between herself and Jeffrey—but he outweighed the latter by at least a stone. Which was not to say that Gilbert was plump; he could better be described as . . . Kate cast about for the proper adjective and eventually selected "square." His torso appeared to form a straight line from his shoulders to his hips, and his legs— tightly encased in a pair of white pantaloons— resembled two sturdy young tree trunks.

"Yes," the earl went on, "Papa often joked about his height. He remarked that had he had the good fortune to be born French, he might well have become emperor in Napoleon's stead. He had a marvelous sense of humor. But I daresay you recollect that, Kate."

She could not continue her deception another instant, Kate thought frantically. She must announce at once that she wasn't Kate Sinclair and had never met Lord Halstead—

"Let us continue our chat in the dining room," Lady Latimer said. "If we delay dinner any longer, the food will grow cold, and Adams will be excessively vexed. Come along."

She hurried toward the archway on the right side of the vestibule, Gilbert and Jeffrey striding behind her and Kate trudging in their wake. Two footmen rushed forward to seat them, then served steaming bowls of soup from a great tureen on the sideboard. Her ladyship started asking Gilbert about various of their mutual friends, and Kate, her mind churning, absently stirred her soup.

She must reveal the truth, of course, but upon reflection, she fancied it would be best to speak with Gilbert in private. Best for him—he would naturally be somewhat embarrassed to learn that Kitty had rejected him—and, Kate owned, best for herself as well. If the earl had inherited his father's celebrated sense of humor, he would probably view her brief, ill-fated impersonation as a magnificent jest. Indeed, he would probably offer to accompany her when she confessed her masquerade to Lady Latimer, and the two of them together could surely persuade her ladyship that Kate had intended no harm.

She drew a tiny sigh of relief and raised a spoonful of soup to her mouth. It was mulligatawny, excellently prepared, and she realized she was ravenous. She swallowed the first spoonful and greedily dipped up another.

"How rude of me!" Lady Latimer said. "Here I

am, talking with Gilbert about people I scarcely know, and I haven't even inquired after your father. I trust Cousin Robert is well?"

Kate choked on her soup. She had not yet told an outright lie, but if she disclosed the current state of Mr. Sinclair's health, she would be compelled to divulge her imposture. She clapped her napkin to her mouth and gulped down the soup, groping for a response.

"He was when last I saw him," she replied at last. "We dined together the night before I sailed, and he was in very high spirits indeed."

"I do wish he had elected to accompany you." Her ladyship sighed. "Well, I fancy he will join us shortly, and in the interim, we are faced with the happy prospect of a very busy Season. We shall be going to Almack's tomorrow evening . . ."

Kate had no notion what Almack's was, but she collected from Lady Latimer's subsequent discourse that it was some sort of dancing club. Her ladyship went on to describe the other activities on their schedule—a ball at the home of Lady This, a rout at General That's, a performance at the King's Theater—and Kate could not quell a stab of bitter regret. It was precisely the life she'd dreamed of, and were it not for the awkward matter of Gilbert, her dreams would be at the very point of fulfillment.

The footmen had brought the entrees by now, and Kate stabbed her veal with frustration. If only the situation were reversed! she thought, her eyes shifting from Gilbert to Jeffrey. The earl was attractive and seemed pleasant enough, but he didn't snatch her breath away or set her heart to pounding. If Jeffrey was Kitty Sinclair's fiancé, Kate could proceed with her charade, win his affection . . .

Jeffrey looked up, his own eyes sweeping her

face, and Kate hastily returned her attention to her plate. He wasn't betrothed to Kitty Sinclair, and—the most bitter regret of all—he would undoubtedly decline to associate with Kate Morrow. He and Lady Latimer might forgive her deception, but they could hardly be expected to include her in the forthcoming festivities. Remembering the biblical injunction to eat, drink, and be merry while one could, Kate wolfed down the veal and the tender new potatoes and a goodly portion of the cauliflower, which she didn't even like.

"And that brings us to my assembly," her ladyship concluded. "Which will be held the first of June." She finished her raspberry tart and sat back, beaming round the table.

"I am certain your ball will be the highlight of the Season, Aunt Jane," Gilbert said politely.

Aunt Jane? It had not occurred to Kate that he might also be a relative.

"It is kind of you to say so, dear." Lady Latimer gave him a fond smile. "But I daresay we have discussed our social calendar long enough. I'm sure you and Kate would welcome a chance to speak alone. Come along, Jeffrey."

She patted her lips and laid her napkin on the tablecloth, and the footmen scurried forward to assist her and Jeffrey from their chairs. They stepped through the archway, and as they disappeared from view, Adams discreetly ushered the footmen out the rear door of the dining room. It had happened so quickly that Kate was at a loss for words, and she took refuge in a great sip of coffee. Unfortunately, the coffee was still extremely hot, and she was hard put not to wince as it scalded her tongue and burned its way down her throat.

"Did you note Aunt Jane's definition of a *discus-*

sion?" Gilbert chuckled. "She talks, and everyone else is required to listen. I can scarcely conceive of two sisters more unlike than she and my mother. Mama was very quiet . . ."

That resolved one mystery, Kate thought. Gilbert was Lady Latimer's nephew—no blood relation to the Sinclairs.

". . . but whenever Aunt Jane's prattle begins to drive me mad, I remind myself what a wonderful woman she is." The earl sketched a fond smile of his own. "I was just a boy when my mother died, and I could not have asked a better substitute than Aunt Jane. I daresay Jeffrey would tell you the same thing."

The same thing? Kate knit her brows. Could Gilbert and Jeffrey be brothers? No, her ladyship had clearly indicated that Jeffrey was a cousin. But perhaps he, too, was connected to Lady Latimer rather than her late husband.

"A wonderful woman indeed," Gilbert continued. "It's a pity she wasn't blessed with children of her own. Though she can be quite as impossible as a natural mother. She is forever meddling in Jeffrey's and my affairs." He emitted another chuckle. "And now it is your turn. Aunt Jane has been eagerly awaiting your arrival since the day Papa returned from Bermuda. She sees Jeffrey and me as the sons she never had, and you will soon be the daughter. She'll torture you with questions and make your life a misery, but you'll come to adore her nonetheless."

He was a fine one to criticize Lady Latimer, Kate reflected wryly: he had talked without visibly pausing for breath since the moment they'd been left alone. She was inclined to let him rattle on forever, but she recognized that the longer she postponed her confession, the more difficult it would be.

"Your aunt has been wonderful to me as well," she murmured. Her throat was still burning a bit, and she coughed to clear it. "However, I must tell you that—"

"That you are shocked not to find me in black gloves." Gilbert heaved a deep sigh. "I feared you would be, but that was Papa's dying wish. Well, not his *dying* wish; he died very suddenly. I fancy Aunt Jane advised you of the circumstances."

"Yes, but—"

"But Papa didn't believe in mourning. He was back in society two weeks after Mama's death, and when I was older, he exacted my promise that I shouldn't mourn him either."

"I understand," Kate said. "But—"

"And if he could have voiced a dying wish, I am confident it would have been the same." The earl flew on. "Indeed, I daresay he would have been even more insistent. He was most taken with you, and he would have wanted you to enjoy your first London Season to the fullest."

"Perhaps so. But—"

"But you are concerned about our wedding plans." Gilbert dropped his eyes to the tablecloth and cleared his own throat. "On that head—"

"No!" Kate croaked. "That is what I have been attempting to explain. I am not—"

"How delighted I am to hear you say so!" The earl's eyes darted up, and he flashed a brilliant smile of relief. "I am not prepared to rush into the parson's mousetrap either."

"No, you still don't understand—"

"Of course I do," he interposed soothingly. "In fact, I suspect we share exactly the same opinion. Arranged marriages have no place in this modern age, do you not concur? But Papa's and Mama's parents arranged their marriage, and Papa always claimed they were happier than most couples who had wed for love. I fancy your father had a similar experience."

Kate hadn't the vaguest notion how Mr. Sinclair might have selected his bride, but she lacked the energy to tender another objection. Gilbert would merely cut her off again—

"At any rate," the earl continued, "Papa made the agreement entirely without my knowledge. Well, not *entirely*," he amended. "I did know he had gone to Bermuda with the specific intention of meeting you and your father. Indeed, I was present when Uncle Horace proposed the idea. And I knew that if everything went well, Papa would explore the possibility of a match between us. But I did not expect to be presented with a fait accompli."

Nor had she, Kate thought grimly.

"At any rate," he repeated, "I do not regard the agreement as binding."

"You . . . you don't?" she stammered.

"Which is not to imply that I take it *lightly*." He hastened on, evidently misconstruing her confusion. "I should very much like to abide by Papa's wishes, and I am in hopes we shall find ourselves compatible. But in the event we do not, I believe either of us should feel free to cry off. I certainly shouldn't sue you for breach of promise, and I trust your father would be equally forgiving. I daresay he would inasmuch as I'm of considerably less value to him now than I was a year ago."

"Value?" Kate echoed.

"I am referring to my title. When our fathers discussed the match, your papa was excessively eager to wed you to a peer. Now, of course, he is a peer himself, and dozens of titled young men would be pleased to court the daughter of a wealthy viscount."

Kate wondered if Jeffrey was numbered among those dozens. Did he possess a title as well? She didn't know, and it really didn't signify; unlike Gilbert and the late Lord Halstead, she could never bring herself to marry for wealth and position alone.

"Therefore," the earl concluded, "my suggestion is that we give ourselves time to become acquainted. If we decide we can be happy together, we shall proceed with our wedding plans, and if not, we shall go our separate ways."

He fell silent at last and gazed expectantly across the table. It was the opportunity Kate had been awaiting—the first and final chance to confess her deception. But her tongue remained frozen to the roof of her mouth, for Gilbert had unwittingly proposed a splendid solution to her dilemma. Indeed, it was the perfect solution: she could continue her masquerade after all and eventually, regretfully terminate their engagement. And what would be the harm? The voice of temptation resumed its insidious whispering. The earl himself had stated that he attached little importance to the nuptial agreement, and if she took care not to encourage his attentions, he was unlikely to fall in love with her. Meanwhile, as she had calculated earlier, she and Jeffrey would often be thrown together—

"Do you concur?" Gilbert said.

"Uh . . . yes." Kate's tongue was still a trifle thick, and she gingerly licked her lips. "Yes, your suggestion is excellent. We shall give ourselves a month or two—"

"A month or two?" He frowned. "Apparently Aunt Jane neglected to tell you."

"Tell me what?" Kate asked warily. She had been presented with enough surprises for one day.

"That she intends to announce our engagement

at her ball. If we request a postponement, she will count it her duty to undertake the personal supervision of our courtship." He shuddered. "It would be vastly better if we could reach a decision before the assembly."

The ball was nearly three weeks away, Kate recalled, and if she did not secure Jeffrey's interest by then, it was doubtful she ever would. "Yes." She nodded. "Yes, I am sure that would be better."

"If we are in agreement then, I shall bid you good night. I daresay your long journey has left you exhausted."

The earl rose, and as he stepped around the table, Kate stood up as well. He stopped beside her, took her hand, and his brows knit another frown.

"I really did anticipate that you would be much taller," he mused. "Papa was quite definite in that regard. In fact, he was somewhat concerned that you might be taller than I. And"—his frown deepened—"he indicated that your eyes were green. I should term them *blue*-green. Perhaps closer to blue."

"They . . . they look green in certain lights," Kate muttered.

"Then I shall look forward to observing them in those lights. I always did fancy green eyes." He dropped her and hand swept a courtly bow.

"Shall I see you tomorrow night?" Kate said politely. "At . . ." She paused and struggled to recollect the name. "At Almack's?"

"I fear not." He shook his head. "I am committed to dine with my aunt. My other aunt," he elaborated as Kate made a moue of puzzlement. "Aunt Agnes is Papa's maiden sister, and she felt his passing very hard."

"I understand." Kate stifled a sigh of relief.

"However, if you are agreeable, I should like to
call Thursday morning and show you round
London. Nine o'clock, shall we say?"

"Yes," Kate murmured. "Nine o'clock will be
fine."

"Till Thursday then."

Gilbert bowed again and strode into the
vestibule, and Kate stared after him, realizing that
the die was irrevocably cast.

5

Until the day she sailed from St. George's harbor,
Kate had never ventured more than twenty miles
from the site of her birth, but despite this
geographic restriction, she doubted many young
women had lived in a wider variety of circumstances. For the first ten years of her life, she had
occupied what most Englishmen would probably
have termed a hut—a thatched cottage consisting
of a single large room, with a curtained alcove at
one end where Mama and Papa slept. Accustomed
to these primitive accommodations, Kate judged
her and Papa's new stone house in Hamilton the
very essence of luxury: though the main room
served as drawing room, dining room, and
kitchen, she and her father had separate bedchambers.

After Papa's death, Kate realized that their
second home was but a scant cut above the first,
for Mrs. Todhunter's mansion had a separate

room for *everything.* In addition to the saloon and the library and the dining room, there was a conservatory (which seemed an excessively silly affectation in view of Bermuda's mild climate), a music room, a ballroom, and a card room. There was even a smoking room, where the men of the household and gentlemen callers could repair to enjoy their pipes and cigars. Few of these rooms were actually used during Kate's residence because Mrs. Todhunter was rarely well enough to leave her private suite. And the only gentleman caller was Mr. Cottle, who did not smoke.

Lady Latimer's house lay somewhere between the extremes of her previous existence, Kate decided as she proceeded from her bedchamber to the ground story. She had been too distracted the day before to take much note of her surroundings, but this morning she counted five bedrooms on the second floor, versus the dozen or more at Todhunter House. And if the size of her room was any indication, the bedchambers were so small as to border on cramped.

As were the public rooms on the first story, she saw, pausing in the corridor to glance through the doorways. The drawing room was scarcely larger than the main room of her and Papa's house in Hamilton; it would have fit twice, with yards to spare, in Mrs. Todhunter's saloon. But the drawing room looked enormous in comparison to those on the opposite side of the hall, where someone—evidently counting the number of rooms more important than their utility—had chopped the available space into two tiny parlors with a music room between them. Inasmuch as the piano filled the latter virtually from wall to wall, Kate was hard put to imagine how any musical entertainment could be conducted. Perhaps the guests would sit in the parlors and listen to an invisible pianist playing his or her tunes through the walls.

Kate descended to the ground floor and turned in the direction of the dining room, calculating that the breakfast parlor would be situated nearby. In fact, Mrs. Todhunter's breakfast parlor had been located immediately behind her dining room, and when Kate reached the archway, she stopped again and peered about. She soon collected that there *was* no breakfast parlor, for the dining-room table was set for three, and an assortment of bowls and platters was arrayed upon the sideboard. As there were no servants in attendance, she further surmised that one was supposed to serve oneself, and she crossed the room, filled a plate, and poured a cup of coffee.

She had heaped her plate fairly to overflowing, Kate noticed as she placed it on the table, and she felt a stab of guilt. Following her conversation with Gilbert, she had realized that she would be compelled to reside with Lady Latimer for some time to come. Her ladyship believed Kate and the earl to be engaged, assumed they would wed in the near future, and she would judge it most peculiar if Kate undertook to lease a house. But she would find some way to make amends, Kate thought, sinking into her chair. And the arrangement did have one splendid advantage: she and Jeffrey would be living under the same roof—

"Good morning, Kate."

It was his voice, Jeffrey's voice, and she started and spun her head. He was striding through the archway, and with a pleasant nod, he advanced to the sideboard and snatched up a plate. He was clad in a moss-green coat this morning, she observed, gazing at his back, and she fancied it couldn't suit him half so well as the brown one he had worn the previous evening. But when he finished serving himself and turned back to face her, she saw that his white waistcoat was edged in gold, exactly matching his pantaloons and complementing his remarkable amber eyes. He took the chair across from hers and laid his napkin in his lap.

"You needn't have waited for me," he said, picking up his fork. "You must be exceedingly hungry."

He glanced at her plate, raising his brows a bit, and Kate noted that they were slightly darker than his hair—brown untinged with any hint of gold. Her cheeks warmed, and she sketched an embarrassed smile.

"I . . . I don't always eat so much," she stammered. "I was seasick during much of the voyage."

"I am sorry to hear that." Jeffrey shook his head with sympathy. "I intended to inquire about your journey last night, but it's difficult to get a word in edgewise when Cousin Jane is present. She drives me to the point of homicide at least once a week, but at the last instant, I remember that she has the soul of a saint."

He flashed a grin of his own, and Kate noticed that he had excellent teeth.

"Gilbert feels the same way," she said. "He mentioned that La . . ." She had momentarily forgotten her role, and she affected a cough. ". . . that Cousin Jane has been a second mother to you both."

"So she has." Jeffrey nodded and swallowed a forkful of scrambled eggs. "Mama died when I was ten—"

"So did mine!" Kate interposed, eagerly seizing on this similarity in their backgrounds.

"Then I was misinformed." Jeffrey frowned. "I was told that your mother died when you were three."

"Yes," Kate hastily agreed.

She must be more careful, she chided herself, must not confuse her own history with that of Kitty Sinclair. Which was easier said than done, for she knew almost nothing of Kitty's life.

"I . . . I meant," she stumbled on, "that we both lost our mothers at an early age."

"Umm." Jeffrey bobbed his head again. "I wonder which of us was better off. After Mama's death, Cousin Jane and Cousin Horace virtually adopted me. I spent all my school holidays with them, and I daresay they were more attentive than the great majority of parents. But you had your father, and my papa was hard put to stay in the same place for two consecutive weeks. He would disappear for days on end even while Mama was alive, and when she was gone . . ."

He stopped and devoured a rasher of bacon. "Suffice it to say," he resumed, "that Papa had been nearly round the world by the time he died. In fact, he'd returned from a two-year excursion to Australia just a week before his death. I count it most ironic that he survived his many adventures only to perish within half a mile of his childhood home. And more ironic yet that he was killed in a riding accident. Papa was a splendid horseman, and Tansy was an old, reliable mare. But there was a storm that day, and evidently she was frightened by a bolt of lightning. She ran him squarely into a tree."

"I am sorry," Kate murmured.

"It happened years ago," he said philosophically. "While I was still up at Oxford. I've since come to wonder if there was a lesson in his death."

"What lesson is that?"

"That though one might travel a million miles, he cannot escape his destiny."

He sounded like Captain Forbes, and Kate experienced a familiar shiver. Had it been her destiny to meet Jeffrey? Her appetite evaporated, but she fancied it would appear excessively odd if she pushed her untouched plate away. She picked up her knife and cut her bilberry muffin in two.

"Papa didn't travel a million miles, of course," Jeffrey went on. "But he did journey to every continent before he died, and you may be pleased to learn that his fondest memories were those of Bermuda. Of his visit to Cousin Robert."

He grinned again and gazed expectantly across the table, and Kate's knife slipped through her fingers and clattered onto her plate. This was a complication she hadn't anticipated, and her mind churned in calculation. She could only make matters worse if she pretended to recollect the visit, she decided, for she knew absolutely nothing of Jeffrey's father. Indeed, when it came to that, she did not even know Jeffrey's surname.

"I fear I don't remember," she muttered.

"Remember?" His expectant look turned to one of puzzlement. "Naturally, you do not *remember*; Papa went to Bermuda long before either of us was born. But I am sure Cousin Robert told you of their grand escapade."

"I . . . I'm afraid not," she gulped.

"How very odd." Jeffrey knit another frown. "Papa told me the story so often that I fancied I should die of boredom. Though I found it terribly exciting the first dozen times I heard it." He emitted a wry chuckle. "Two young men charging out in hot pursuit of the Americans who had stolen all the gunpowder in Bermuda . . ."

He proceeded to describe the theft, but Kate had heard the story dozens of times herself: next to the

wreck of the original colonists, the American raid on
the powder magazine was perhaps the most
significant event in Bermudian history. It had
occurred in 1775, she recalled; and if her estimate of
Mr. Sinclair's age was correct, he would, in fact,
have been quite young—not much above twenty.

". . . and until the day of his death," Jeffrey was
saying, "Papa claimed that he and Cousin Robert
were the only men on the island who actually
witnessed the incident. They reached the magazine
just as the last boats were rowing out to the frigate
offshore . . ."

The only men prepared to *admit* they had
witnessed the incident, Kate thought. It was
Bermuda's shameful, open secret that factions
within the colony had directly or indirectly abetted
the raid.

". . . so they appropriated a fishing boat"—
Jeffrey chuckled again—"and they were within a
hundred yards of the frigate when their rudder
broke. Which was fortunate for them because they
would have been in a wretched coil if they'd caught
the warship up. They had consumed a considerable
excess of spirits before they set out, and in later
years, Papa regarded their chase as a marvelous
prank. I doubt the Americans would have viewed it
in such an innocuous light."

Though Kate had listened to him only intermit-
tently, she had registered the gist of his narrative
—more than enough to "remember" that her father
had related the story after all. But if she affected to
recollect one tale, he might well bring up another.

"They grew quite close," Jeffrey said, "and they
continued to correspond until Papa's death. In jest,
Cousin Robert always directed his letters to 'Uncle
Alfred.' They thought it quite hilarious that though

they were but a few months apart in age, your father was my father's nephew."

Having had no aunts, uncles, or cousins of her own, Kate often found it difficult to puzzle out family relationships; but at length, she concluded that Alfred must have been the brother of Mr. Sinclair's father. There was no other explanation: had he been connected to Mr. Sinclair on his mother's side, Lady Latimer would not regard Jeffrey as a cousin. Mr. Sinclair had stated that his father was the second son of a viscount, she recalled, and apparently Jeffrey's father was the third. Since he was so much younger than his siblings, Kate further speculated that he was the son of a second marriage. But she dared not ask, for it was something Kitty Sinclair would know.

"How very odd," Jeffrey repeated. "I can scarcely believe Cousin Robert didn't mention their great adventure."

His amber eyes narrowed, flickered, and Kate's heart leapt into her throat. Had she aroused his suspicions? She was casting about for some credible way to explain her ignorance when his face cleared.

"But perhaps I shouldn't be surprised," he said. "I tend to forget that Cousin Robert was approaching middle age when you were born. He was almost forty, and unlike my own father"—his smile was bitter round the edges—"Cousin Robert had become a highly respectable citizen. I daresay he was reluctant to discuss his youthful follies."

"I . . . I daresay so," Kate nervously agreed.

"I sometimes wonder what would have happened if they'd met again later in life," Jeffrey mused. "They followed such different paths that I wonder if their friendship could have survived. But let us say no more about our fathers." Kate judged this a monstrous good idea. "I've given you no chance to tell me about your journey. Were you seasick all the way from Bermuda?"

"Not all the way."

She described the arduous voyage of the *Queen Anne*—except, of course, for the captain's view that their troubles had been caused by Mr. Sinclair's recently departed spirit. Jeffrey continued to eat as she spoke, and when she had finished, he moved his plate aside and sat back in his chair.

"It is fortunate you were delayed no longer," he said. "Gilbert was extremely anxious to meet you, and he was growing quite wild with impatience. I am sure he now counts the wait well-justified."

His eyes swept her face, and Kate's cheeks began to flame again.

"I trust you are equally pleased?" Jeffrey added.

He had introduced another complication, and Kate belatedly realized it was one she should have foreseen. Jeffrey would naturally be reluctant to initiate a courtship if he believed her firmly committed to Gilbert, and she groped for the proper, discreet reply.

"Gilbert is very pleasant," she murmured at length. "But—"

"How lovely!" Lady Latimer sailed through the archway, clasping her hands with delight. "It warms my heart to see the two of you together. Your fathers were such dear friends. I know they would be thrilled if you formed a similar friendship." She beamed back and forth between them.

"Nothing would please me more," Jeffrey said.

His eyes danced over Kate's face again, and she felt the threat of still another blush.

"At the moment, however"—he laid his napkin on the table—"I am already overdue at Brooks's. So if you will excuse me . . ."

He rose and stepped to Lady Latimer's side, kissed her cheek, bowed to Kate, and proceeded into the foyer. He briefly disappeared from Kate's view, and when he reappeared, he was clapping a beaver hat on his head; evidently he had left it in the entry hall. He strode toward the door, once more passing out of Kate's sight, and she soon heard the click of the latch.

"Is Brooks a friend of Jeffrey's?" she asked as the door slammed closed. She was compelled to call the question over her shoulder, for Lady Latimer was serving herself at the sideboard.

"A friend?" Her ladyship laughed. "No, dear, Brooks's is one of the premier men's clubs in London." She reappeared as well and sank into the chair at the head of the table. "Men!" She rolled her eyes in despair. "They claim their clubs are centers of intellectual discussion, but in truth, the principal activity is gaming. And poor Jeffrey doesn't even care for gaming. But he goes there day after day, attempting to maintain a brave facade . . ."

She sobered, heaved a sigh, and gazed into the empty vestibule. "He is such a fine young man," she resumed, looking back at her plate.

"Yes, he is," Kate concurred with a sigh of her own. "And Gilbert too," she added quickly as Lady Latimer glanced up. "I collect that both of them have been like sons to you."

"So they have." Her ladyship nodded. "Had I been blessed with sons of my own, I could not have hoped for better ones. Though I cannot but reflect that matters would have been vastly simpler if Horace and I *had* had a son. There would have been no question about the inheritance, and as it was . . ." Her voice trailed off.

"As it was?" Kate pressed.

"Umm." Evidently Lady Latimer had also lost

her appetite: she replaced her fork on her plate and shoved the plate away. "Since there seems no delicate way to phrase it, I shall have to beg your forgiveness. Horace always assumed he would outlive your father. You may recall that Horace was three years the younger to begin with and could be expected to survive Cousin Robert even in normal circumstances. And Horace judged the circumstances in Bermuda far from normal. He counted it likely that Cousin Robert would contract a fever or perish in a hurricane . . ." She stopped again and tendered an apologetic smile.

As well she should, Kate thought. It was, indeed, a most indelicate subject, and she could not conceive why her ladyship had brought it up.

"At any rate," Lady Latimer went on, "when Jeffrey came down from Oxford, he was naturally concerned about his future. He spoke of seeking a career in the army or emigrating to one of the colonies, but Horace would have none of that. He didn't want an untrained soldier or adventurer to take his place, Horace said; he wanted Jeffrey to become familiar with the properties and responsibilities he would ultimately inherit."

Inherit? Dear God. Kate's mouth went dry. She had fancied there would be no harm in her impersonation, but she had failed to consider—

"So Jeffrey abandoned his plans," her ladyship continued. "He consented to assist Horace in the administration of the Latimer estates, and now . . . Well, you know what happened. Horace predeceased your father after all, and Cousin Robert became Viscount Latimer. And dear Jeffrey has been left quite at loose ends."

How could she have overlooked such a critical point? Kate wondered frantically. She understood the laws of inheritance all too well: her own granduncle's title and estate had passed to a distant cousin. A cousin Mama didn't even know, but he was Sir Randolph Edgerton's nearest male relative. Kate should have remembered that there was someone—some man—standing next behind Mr. Sinclair in the line to succeed Lord Latimer. Had it not been Jeffrey, it would have been someone else, but in the event . . .

"Jeffrey!" she moaned. "I have stolen his inheritance."

"What nonsense!" Lady Latimer said crisply. "Jeffrey was fully aware of the situation when he agreed to Horace's proposal. I mentioned the matter only because I wished to be sure you understood as well."

'But I—"

"And let us be realistic," her ladyship interjected. "At the risk of further indelicacy, I must point out that Cousin Robert cannot live forever. He has passed sixty, and it seems highly improbable he will wed again and sire a son at this late juncture. Within five years, ten at the outside, Jeffrey will have his legacy. He is barely one-and-thirty; he can afford to wait."

"But . . ."

Kate registered the import of Lady Latimer's words, and her protest died on her tongue. Far from harming Jeffrey, her masquerade could be greatly to his advantage. She had already calculated that months might elapse before Mr. Sinclair's English relatives learned of his death, and she was in a position to convey the news whenever she chose. She need only write herself a letter and pretend it came from Bermuda. From Samuel Wilcox, she decided; it would be entirely natural for Mr. Sinclair's business partner to notify her of her father's sudden demise.

Indeed, Kate reflected with growing excitement, such a course would serve to kill two birds with a single stone. Jeffrey would succeed to his inheritance at once, and in view of Kate's tragic loss, the announcement of her engagement to Gilbert would be indefinitely postponed. In fact, Lady Latimer would probably cancel her assembly altogether. Which hardly seemed fair inasmuch as her ladyship had just shed her widow's weeds . . .

Kate wrinkled her forehead and glimpsed a splendid solution to this dilemma as well. She would "receive" the communication from Mr. Wilcox the day before Lady Latimer's ball and—borrowing a leaf from Gilbert's book—bravely insist that her father would have wanted the assembly to proceed. Though she herself, Kate would add, was much too distraught to contemplate wedding plans until she recovered from her shock.

"Please don't frown so, dear," Lady Latimer said. "I know what you are thinking."

Kate's eyes darted to the head of the table. Mrs. Todhunter's gargantuan black cook had professed an ability to read minds and foretell the future, and her pronouncements had proved uncannily accurate on more than one occasion. But Delilah had always appeared to sink into a trance when she experienced second sight, and Lady Latimer merely looked kind.

"You are wondering if Jeffrey can also afford to wait in the financial sense," her ladyship elaborated. "I am happy to assure you he can. His maternal grandfather was exceedingly wealthy, and he possessed the good sense to put most of Louisa's dowry in trust for their children. For Louisa and Alfred's children, I mean. Had the money gone directly to Alfred, I daresay it would have been frittered away before the honeymoon was over."

"Yes," Kate murmured. "Jeffrey indicated that his father was rather irresponsible."

"Poor Alfred." Lady Latimer shook her head. "He was not an evil person; he simply failed to grow up. I fancy his wildness came from his mother. Your great-grandfather's second wife. Cousin Robert no doubt explained that she was an actress prior to their marriage."

"Umm," Kate grunted.

"Fortunately, Jeffrey shows no trace of her influence," her ladyship went on. "Though he physically resembles his father, he inherited Louisa's excellent character. He was involved in his share of boyhood scrapes, of course, but apart from that . . ." She sketched her familiar fond smile. "At any rate, I promise you he harbors no ill will toward you or Cousin Robert either one."

Not at present, Kate thought, and if she were careful, he never would. At the proper time, she would confess her deception, but by then, she would have won Jeffrey's heart and cleverly delivered his legacy. She drew a small sigh of relief and returned her attention to Lady Latimer.

". . . occurs to me," her ladyship was saying, "that as you were not familiar with Brooks's, you probably know nothing of Almack's either."

"Nothing beyond what you said last night," Kate agreed, judging it safe to own to ignorance. "I collect it is some sort of dancing club."

"A dancing club?" Lady Latimer's horrified expression suggested that Kate had equated the established Church to a heathen religious cult. "It is much more than that, my dear. If one cannot obtain a voucher of admission to Almack's, one might as well be dead. Lady Jersey is the most influential woman in Britain."

Lady Jersey. Another name. Kate's relief disintegrated, and her head began to ache. Should she know who Lady Jersey was?

"Lady Jersey is the principal patroness of Almack's." Lady Latimer answered her unasked question. "And I cannot emphasize too strongly the importance of creating a favorable impression when you meet her. As Gilbert's wife, you will naturally be accepted in society, but Lady Jersey determines who is *ton* and who is not. If she likes you, your road will be an easy one, but if she doesn't . . ."

Lady Latimer's lips thinned to a grim line; apparently the alternative was too awful to be voiced aloud.

"I understand," Kate said.

"Of course you do, and I am sure Lady Jersey will like you very much indeed." Lady Latimer extended one arm along the table, but she was situated too far away to pat Kate's shoulder, so she patted the lace cloth instead. "Be certain to wear your best gown and be on your best behavior. Not that you would ever behave *badly*, but you must be especially courteous to Lady Jersey . . ."

She chattered on, and Kate's headache grew to a dull, relentless throb. Though Lady Latimer undoubtedly had a heart of gold, her incessant prattle *was* enough to drive one to the point of murder. But homicide would hardly be construed as "best behavior," and at length, Kate retrieved her knife and reduced her uneaten muffin to crumbs.

6

". . . and this," Lady Latimer said nervously, "is my dear cousin, Miss Catherine Sinclair. The daughter of Horace's cousin, that is. The one who is now Viscount Latimer."

"It is a pleasure to make your acquaintance, Miss Sinclair."

Lady Jersey granted Kate a cool nod, and Kate studied "the most influential woman in Britain" from beneath her lashes. The countess (Lady Latimer had mentioned during the drive to King Street that she was a countess) was older than Kate had expected—sixty at least and possibly several years beyond. But she was still prodigious handsome, and Kate could readily understand why she had once been the Regent's mistress. (Or so it was rumored; Lady Latimer had supplied that *on-dit* during the drive as well.) Time had taken its inevitable toll, of course: there was a web of fine lines around Lady Jersey's eyes, and deep grooves extended from the edges of her nostrils to the corners of her tiny, heart-shaped mouth. As if to divert attention from these deficiencies, her ladyship was clad in a dramatic black gown, adorned with dozens of crepe roses and hundreds of jet beads—

Lady Latimer kicked Kate's ankle, and she repressed a wince and glanced up.

"I . . . I am pleased to meet you too," she stammered.

"You were bred up in Bermuda, I believe?"

Lady Jersey's tone was perfectly polite, but she

was inspecting Kate's dress in turn, and Kate
looked self-consciously down again. In accordance
with Lady Latimer's instructions, she had worn
her best gown—the yellow muslin trimmed in
white lace—but she was beginning to fear it was
hopelessly old-fashioned. The high, square neck
bore no resemblance to the plunging corsages of
Lady Jersey's and Lady Latimer's dresses; the
sleeves were too loose and much too long; and the
skirt ended just below her shins—

Lady Latimer pinched her arm, and Kate hastily
returned her attention to Lady Jersey.

"Yes," she replied, "I was born and bred up in
Bermuda."

"It's a pity Lord Latimer could not accompany
you to England." Lady Jersey's expression was
one of regret, but her tone was now tinged ever so
subtly with disapproval. How could a British peer
be so careless of his responsibilities?

"There was some confusion on that head," Lady
Latimer said quickly. "Cousin Robert was not
aware of Horace's death at the time Kate sailed. I
daresay he will join us as soon as he learns of his
inheritance."

Kate was seized by a fit of coughing, and Jeffrey,
who was standing at her other side, pounded her
solicitiously on the back.

"He will surely come for the wedding?" Lady
Jersey arched her feathery brows. "I am given to
understand you will shortly wed young Halstead."

It was scarcely surprising that her ladyship was
so powerful, Kate thought dryly; apparently she
knew the whereabouts and plans of every
remotely important person in the empire.

"That is not yet official." Lady Latimer once
more responded in Kate's stead. "However, it was
Daniel's fondest wish, his *dying* wish, and I hope

there will be a betrothal announcement in the near future."

"And what of you, Mr. Sinclair?" Lady Jersey shifted her eyes to Jeffrey. "Will this be the year you take a wife as well?"

"That remains to be seen," he said politely.

"Where *is* Miss Dalton this evening?" The countess peered past him and essayed a pretty frown.

Miss Dalton? Kate's heart crashed against her ribs. Who was Miss Dalton?

"Still in Hampshire," Jeffrey said.

"Ah, yes, I recollect that her mother has been ill. A stomach complaint, I believe."

"Yes." A wry note had crept into Jeffrey's voice. "However, Mrs. Dalton was much improved when I myself left Hampshire, and I anticipate Barbara's arrival any day."

"Excellent," Lady Jersey cooed. "Perhaps we can also anticipate an announcement of your engagement before the Season is over."

"You will certainly be the first to know," he said solemnly.

His comment was clearly a double entendre, and the countess flushed a bit.

"I fancy I have monopolized you long enough," she snapped. "The other patronesses are eager to meet Miss Sinclair."

Lady Latimer nodded and beckoned Kate on along the receiving line. Barbara? Kate silently echoed, clenching her hands with dismay. She muttered a greeting to Countess Lieven. Engagement? She acknowledged her introduction to Lady Sefton. Was Jeffrey at the very point of wedding someone else? She desperately wanted to ask Lady Latimer, but when they reached the end of the receiving line, her ladyship tugged Kate into the main ballroom and began ushering her from one knot of guests to another. This, Lady Latimer happily announced to all, was her "dear little cousin" from Bermuda . . .

Within the space of half an hour, Kate had been presented to so many lords and ladies, so many generals and colonels and honorables, that she could not keep count of them, much less remember their names. It was exactly the sort of scene she'd imagined when she had dreamed of removing to England, and she supposed she should be fairly wild with excitement. But the specter of Miss Dalton hovered like a great black cloud over the glittering throng in the ballroom. What was she like? Kate wondered. Tall? Short? Thin? Fat? Blonde? Brunette? Was she beautiful? Rich? Had Jeffrey known her for many years? Perhaps she was his childhood sweetheart—

"You must not take it so seriously," Jeffrey said.

For a moment, Kate collected that he—like Delilah—was reading her mind, and she started. But when her eyes darted to his face, he flashed a sardonic grin and shook his head. They were alone, she observed; Lady Latimer was some yards away, chatting with Lord and Lady Kemble. Kemble or Kendall or maybe Kimber—

"You appear to be in a fog," Jeffrey went on, "and you will never succeed if you allow them to intimidate you." He waved vaguely round the ballroom. "Beneath their finery, they're quite like all the other human beings in the world. No better and no worse than the people you knew in Bermuda." He paused. "Would you care to stand up with me?"

It was difficult to hear the orchestra above the buzz of conversation, but when Kate tilted one ear toward the balcony, she recognized the strains of a waltz. She had attended a few assemblies just prior to Papa's death, but the waltz had been new then—rarely played—and she had attempted it no more than half a dozen times. She started to say so, then realized she was once more confusing her own history with that of Kitty Sinclair. Four years had elapsed since Kate last set foot on a dance floor, and Kitty had probably attended a ball every week.

"I should be delighted," she murmured. "Though I fear I'm a trifle out of practice."

In the event, this proved to be a monumental understatement: "a trifle out of practice" was far too flattering a phrase to describe Kate's gross ineptitude. She trod on Jeffrey's shoes even as he escorted her to the floor, and matters grew progressively worse as he began to whirl her about. As he began to *try* to whirl her about, she amended grimly. When he guided her backward, she lurched so far as nearly to throw him off balance, and when he pulled her, forward, she stumbled into his chest. Meanwhile she trod on his feet again at least one step in three, and on several occasions, he was unable to quell a grunt of pain. At length, however, Kate adjusted to his rhythm, and when they had succeeded in dancing thirty full seconds without a major mishap, she dared to raise her eyes to his face. He was gazing down at her, his own eyes narrowed.

"I am sorry," she mumbled. "I have never been an accomplished dancer."

"No?" His eyes narrowed a trifle further. "Daniel reported that you were an *extremely* accomplished dancer. He especially enjoyed standing up with you for the boulanger. It was at the governor's assembly, I believe he said."

Another mistake, Kate chided herself; she must learn to think before she spoke. "I meant," she elaborated hastily, "that I am not an accomplished *waltzer.* The waltz is not yet popular in Bermuda."

"No?" Jeffrey repeated. "Daniel didn't mention that. But I daresay he had little opportunity to go to balls. As I recall, he was in Bermuda but a few weeks."

"Umm," Kate muttered. It was imperative to change the subject, and she cast frantically about for an innocuous topic. But the only topic that came to mind was the one which had haunted her for the past three quarters of an hour. "Who is Miss Dalton?" she blurted out.

"A young woman of my acquaintance."

"Yes, I inferred that you are quite *well* acquainted."

His eyes flickered, and Kate belatedly perceived that she had gone too far.

"Or is Lady Jersey an inveterate matchmaker?" she added as lightly as she could.

"She is that." Jeffrey nodded. "In this instance, however . . . Well, there is no point in hiding my teeth. Cousin Jane remarked that Daniel's fondest wish was to see you and Gilbert wed, and I fancy the same could be said of Mr. Dalton. His fondest wish is to wed Barbara to me."

"But why?" Kate pressed.

She recognized even as the words emerged that it was an excessively rude question—suggesting that no sensible father could possibly entertain such a wish. She prayed Jeffrey would let it pass, but he sketched another ironic smile.

"Am I that odious?" he said.

"No! No, I merely wondered . . . You seemed to imply that Mr. Dalton *specifically* wants to wed his daughter to you, and . . . and I wondered why," she concluded lamely.

"For the same reason your father wanted to wed you to Gilbert. In fact"—his eyes now narrowed in reflection—"you and Barbara have a good deal in

common. Her grandfather was also the second son
of a viscount, and he emigrated to America when
Uncle Edwin went to Bermuda. The elder Mr.
Dalton settled in Boston and made a great fortune,
but he was a staunch loyalist, and he returned to
England at the outbreak of the American
rebellion. It was a considerable financial sacrifice,
and he expected his patriotism to be rewarded by
a peerage."

"I see," Kate lied. The American rebellion had
occurred forty years since; what conceivable
bearing could it have on Miss Dalton's present
circumstances?

"But he was not granted a title," Jeffrey went
on, "and though he lived for many years
thereafter, he never recovered from his
disappointment. It was left to his son—Barbara's
father—to rebuild the family fortune, and when
Barbara was born, he vowed to wed her into the
peerage. I chanced to be the first and most
convenient candidate. Mr. Dalton purchased the
estate adjoining Cousin Horace's, and Barbara
and I grew up together. Her father encouraged our
friendship because he assumed I should one day
be a viscount."

He stopped and spun Kate around in silence for
a moment. "As I indicated, the situation differs
only in its particulars from yours. Cousin Robert
arranged your marriage to Gilbert because he
assumed Gilbert would one day be an earl." He
paused again, then emitted a mirthless chuckle. "I
must say that at this juncture, it appears your
father had the better hand."

He *was* bitter, Kate thought dismally. Lady
Latimer's assurances to the contrary, he deeply
resented the loss of his legacy.

"But perhaps Cousin Robert won't agree,"
Jeffrey continued. "When he learns of his

inheritance, he may decide he placed his wager too early. A year ago, he was merely wealthy, and now he is wealthy and titled as well. You could have almost any husband you wished."

"Please, Jeffrey—"

"I am not attempting to dissuade you from wedding Gilbert," he interposed quickly. "You've been exceedingly lucky thus far—you and Cousin Robert both—and you can well afford another gamble."

"Gamble?" Kate shook her head.

"Cousin Robert didn't tell you?" Jeffrey's eyes flickered again, but at length, he bobbed his own head. "I daresay he didn't want to arouse your hopes. Or perhaps Daniel was too discreet to reveal that Gilbert stands to become a marquess."

"A marquess?" Kate echoed weakly. She had barely puzzled out the complex relationships among the Sinclairs and the Halsteads, and he was introducing a further complication.

"The Marquess of Ashbourne," Jeffrey confirmed with another nod. "Gilbert is his third cousin or some such thing. Ashbourne is a relatively young man—forty-five or fifty, I should guess—but he's always been a sickly fellow. He's been married for many years, but he has no children, and it appears increasingly unlikely he will. And if he dies without a son, Gilbert will succeed to the title. Though not to much else, I'm sorry to say. Ashbourne is wretchedly poor—"

"Stop it!" Kate stamped one foot, and Jeffrey instinctively winced. "Is that all you ever think of? Money and position?"

"What do *you* think of?" he countered. "Like it or not, money and position are the cornerstones of society. The ideal circumstance is to possess both, and that is frequently accomplished by marriage.

Your case is an excellent example. At the time your marriage was arranged, your father had nothing but wealth, and Gilbert had prospects of a title."

And his case was the mirror image of hers, Kate reflected: Miss Dalton's father had the wealth, and Jeffrey had the prospects. As Lady Latimer had so indelicately pointed out, "Cousin Robert" could not live forever. Indeed, unbeknownst to anyone but Kate, he had had the good grace to die already. Though she had scarcely been acquainted with Mr. Sinclair, she felt a stir of anger.

"I collect that affection plays no part in it?" she said warmly. "In your . . . your grand scheme to combine money and rank?"

"It is not *my* grand scheme," Jeffrey protested. "It is the way of the world. And fortunately, affection often does play a part. Young people tend to be malleable, and wise parents can manipulate events without seeming to do so. One sees it in London every Season. Miss X is introduced to Mr. Y, and within a few weeks, they have fallen over head and ears in love and inform their families they wish to wed. Which is precisely the goal the parents had in mind when they engineered the introduction in the first place."

"You appear to hold love in very low esteem," Kate snapped.

"Do I?" He looked genuinely surprised. "Then I have created the wrong impression, for the truth is I hold no opinion at all. I have never experienced such an emotion, and I am therefore inclined to doubt it exists. I suspect that love is a lofty synonym for infatuation. When it ends, as it inevitably must, the lucky couple find themselves sufficiently compatible to live together in relative harmony."

"And that is your feeling for Miss Dalton?" Kate once more spoke without thinking. "You find her . . . compatible?"

"She is a pleasant young woman," he responded airily. "I fancy we shall get on well enough if we decide to marry."

And where did that leave her? Kate wondered. "If" was an encouraging word; evidently there was no firm commitment. But it was clear that Jeffrey wasn't the sort to conceive a sudden *tendre* . . . The music stopped, and he released her, bowed his thanks, and ushered her off the floor.

"Here you are at last!" Lady Latimer bounded forward to meet them. "I thought the dance would never end. I wanted to present Kate to the Duke of Cambridge, but you were so absorbed in your conversation that I could not attract your attention. It's fortunate Gilbert isn't here." She cast Jeffrey a frown of mock reproval. "He might conclude that you are attempting to steal his fiancée."

"Steal his fiancée?" Jeffrey flushed with exasperation. "Where *is* Gilbert, by the by?" His voice seemed a trifle overloud.

"Dining with Agnes," her ladyship replied absently, peering over his shoulder. "She has remained quite inconsolable since Daniel's death . . ." She sucked in her breath and seized Kate's wrist. "The duke is free," she hissed. "He has just finished chatting with Lady Kemble. Hurry, dear, before he starts to talk to someone else."

She tugged Kate toward a tall, portly, round-faced man who was gazing vacuously round the ballroom. As they approached his royal highness, Kate glanced over her own shoulder, but Jeffrey had vanished into the crowd.

7

"That is the last portrait of my father." Gilbert indicated a large painting on the wall above the fireplace. "It was finished just a week before he departed for Bermuda."

Kate gazed dutifully up and attempted to study the picture, but her vision was beginning to blur with exhaustion. Indeed, her whole body was exhausted—from her throbbing head to her swollen feet—and she prayed that this interminable day would soon be over.

As promised, Gilbert had called promptly at nine, assisted Kate into his curricle, and announced that the Tower of London would be the first stop on their tour of the city. Kate inferred from this remark that they would proceed directly to the Tower, but the earl paused some half a dozen times en route to point out other sites of interest and explain—at great length—their historical significance. Kate was feeling the initial twinges of a headache well before they reached the Tower, and when she glimpsed its distinctive turrets, she drew a small sigh of relief.

Her relief was short-lived, however, for it soon became apparent that Gilbert's maddening chatter was merely the prelude to an endless series of lectures. After whisking Kate past the crown jewels—the attraction she had most wanted to see—he led her to Tower Hill and darkly reminded her that it had been the scene of seventy-five beheadings and hangings over the years. He began to enumerate the victims, evidently determined to name and describe them all; but when his recital was finished, Kate noted one glaring omission.

"What of Anne Boleyn?" she asked.

Gilbert replied rather testily that the ill-fated queen had been executed on Tower *Green*. He offered to show Kate the spot, but as her feet were starting to ache as well, she declined.

During the drive from the Tower to St. Paul's, Gilbert delivered addresses on the history of the cathedral and the life of Sir Christopher Wren, and Kate optimistically fancied that he could have little more to say when they toured the building. But she was once more doomed to disappointment, for the earl proved to be a veritable fount of esoteric architectural knowledge. Kate did not much care whether a particular window was trefoil, quatrefoil, cinquefoil, or multifoil; and by the time Gilbert ushered her back to the carriage, she cared considerably less.

From St. Paul's, they continued to Westminster Abbey, the earl again supplying a wealth of background information as they drove. Kate was too wise by now to entertain even the faintest hope that he would exhaust his store of facts before they reached their destination, but she could not repress a gasp of dismay when they stepped through the main portal. In addition to the wide variety of architectural features, there were hundreds and hundreds of tombs, and she was grimly certain that Gilbert would insist on seeing every one.

Kate was unable to say how many of the monuments they actually viewed because it required all her concentration to stumble along in Gilbert's wake and hold her head erect while he droned his biographical lectures. At length, however—judging that she was perilously near to death herself—she summoned sufficient strength to suggest they postpone the rest of their tour till another day.

"Umm." The earl plucked a watch from his waistcoat pocket, snapped it open, and peered at the face. "Perhaps we should. It is already half past three."

Kate had estimated that it was much, much later.

"And I want to show you my town house before we return to Aunt Jane's," he added. "I daresay you would welcome a cup of tea."

Kate would have welcomed a long nap far more, but she fancied it would be excessively impolite to say no. And in the event, she did have a brief nap, for she dozed most of the way to Gilbert's house in Welbeck Street. Fortunately, the earl did not appear to notice: each time she started awake, he was happily chattering names and dates and other fascinating historical details.

"What do you think of it?" Gilbert asked, jarring her back to the present.

Kate blinked her eyes into focus and redirected her attention to the portrait. Though the late Lord Halstead was seated in a chair, it was clear he'd been quite short: his feet barely reached the floor, and the back of the chair extended almost to his shoulders. But apart from his diminutive stature, he looked like an older version of his son—the round face a trifle plumper, the fair skin creased here and there with wrinkles, the sandy hair receding at the temples.

"It is an excellent likeness," she murmured.

"Excellent?" Gilbert frowned. "Papa felt it was much too flattering, and I am inclined to agree. Surely you recollect that his hair had gone gray."

"Except for his hair," Kate hastily amended. "I

meant to say that it is an excellent likeness except for the hair."

"Your tea, sir." The butler loomed up in the drawing-room entry, a silver tray in his hands. "Shall I put it on the sofa table?"

"Thank you, Hawkins. Will you pour, Kate?"

She had been perched at one end of the couch, and as she wriggled toward the middle, her backside encountered an obstruction. She glanced down and saw a clump of stuffing poking through a rent in the upholstery. It came as no surprise, for she had observed similar symptoms of decay throughout the house: faded draperies, frayed carpets, hangings peeling from the walls . . . Hawkins set the tea tray on the table, and when Kate leaned forward to pour, she further noted that the silver pot was dented and one of the Wedgwood cups was chipped.

"As I fear you can see for yourself, the house requires a great deal of work."

Gilbert took his cup—the unchipped one—and sank into the Adam armchair on the opposite side of the table. It teetered a bit, and Kate noticed that the left front foot was missing.

"Naturally, you will have full authority to redecorate as you wish," the earl went on. "Immediately after we are wed, we shall refurbish the town house and my estate in Warwickshire as well."

Kate's own cup began to clatter in the saucer, and she quickly raised it to her mouth and sipped from the undamaged part of the rim.

"Which brings up a rather delicate point." Gilbert cleared his throat. "The matter of your dowry."

"My . . . my dowry?" she stammered.

The thought had not occurred to her until that

moment, and she could scarcely believe she had been so obtuse. Jeffrey had repeatedly alluded to a union of Mr. Sinclair's wealth and Gilbert's title; how had she fancied the money would be paid? Had she supposed Gilbert would receive monthly wages for his service as Kitty's husband?

"As I indicated"—the earl emitted another cough—"it is an exceedingly delicate point. I well recognize the impropriety of involving you in the financial aspects of our marriage. However, since your father elected not to accompany you to England, I assume he made an alternative arrangement."

"Alternative arrangement?" Kate repeated.

"Lord Latimer must have appointed someone to conduct the negotiations in his stead." Gilbert sketched a pleasant smile, but his voice was edged with impatience. "A solicitor, I should guess, and I was in hopes you could give me his name."

Negotiations? Kate's head whirled with confusion. Had the amount of the dowry not been decided? She took another sip of tea, and her mind began to clear. She didn't know what had transpired between the late Lord Halstead and the late Lord Latimer, but Gilbert did not expect her to know. It therefore seemed safe to say the truth.

"I was under the impression that the agreement was made while your father was in Bermuda."

"They reached a *basic* agreement, of course." The earl was no longer attempting to disguise his impatience. "A settlement of fifteen thousand pounds. But . . ."

Kate choked on her tea and slammed her cup and saucer on the table. Fifteen thousand pounds! It was three times her legacy from Mrs. Todhunter, and she had counted herself quite prosperous.

". . . details were to be determined later," Gilbert was saying. "The portions that would be in cash and property and investments and so forth."

"I . . . I see." Kate was still sputtering, and she wiped her mouth with one of the tattered linen napkins.

"As I stated, I assume Lord Latimer has engaged a local agent to represent his interests. Or intends to do so. Perhaps he sent a letter with you? He might have neglected to emphasize its urgency."

"N-no." Kate shook her head.

"Then he undoubtedly dispatched a message through the post. I daresay his representative will communicate with me shortly."

Kate started to choke again.

"However . . ."

Gilbert stopped and tendered another smile. Kate surmised that he was trying to look contrite, but his expression more nearly resembled a grimace of pain.

"However," he resumed, "in the event I do not hear from Lord Latimer's agent, our engagement will have to be postponed. I trust you understand that there can be no announcement until the particulars of your dowry have been determined."

"Yes," Kate gulped. "Yes, I quite understand."

"Excellent!" the earl said brightly. "Have you had enough tea?" He replaced his own cup and saucer on the tray. "If so, I did promise Aunt Jane I should have you back by half past five."

He leapt up without awaiting a response, tugged Kate to her feet, and escorted her out of the saloon and down the stairs to the vestibule. There hadn't been time to show her all the many items of interest in the house, he lamented as he propelled her toward the door. The cabinet, for instance—he had not even pointed out the cabinet. He waved at a blackened block of wood against the foyer wall.

It needed some repair, he owned, but it was an extremely valuable antique, dating from the reign of Charles I . . .

"Did I mention that it was Charles the First who created the Halstead earldom?" he asked, handing Kate into the curricle.

"No," she said wearily.

"Yes." He climbed into the carriage and clucked the horses to a start. "He was eager to enlist untitled landowners in the royalist cause . . ."

Kate closed her ears to his dissertation and pondered the "delicate" matter of her dowry. Her initial reaction was one of relief. If there was no communication from Lord Latimer—as, of course, there wouldn't be—Gilbert would cry off the engagement himself, which meant that Kate need not rush to compose a letter from Mr. Wilcox before Lady Latimer's ball. She could wait till the assembly was over, till the Season was over, till the *year* was over . . .

No, she could not, she realized, belatedly perceiving the flaw in her logic. If Gilbert postponed the betrothal announcement, Lady Latimer would demand an explanation, and the earl would be forced to reveal the confusion surrounding the nuptial agreement. Her ladyship might be persuaded that another message had been lost in transit, but Jeffrey's suspicions were sure to be aroused.

In fact, Jeffrey's suspicions might be aroused long before the ball. Kate's stomach fluttered with panic. There was no reason to suppose that Gilbert would hold his tongue until the last minute. To the contrary. He expected to hear from Lord Latimer's representative "shortly," and when he did not, he might well mention his puzzlement to Jeffrey. So perhaps it would be best to "receive" Mr. Wilcox's letter at once . . .

But that course was also fraught with peril. Kate clenched her hands, her mind beginning to churn again. Following her conversation with Jeffrey, she had recognized that her knowledge was a two-edged sword. With a few strokes of the pen, she could give Jeffrey his inheritance, but would that not be to Miss Dalton's advantage? The reality of a title was infinitely more desirable than even the grandest prospects. Mr. Dalton would redouble his efforts to contract a match . . .

Kate's head was still spinning when the curricle stopped in front of Lady Latimer's house. Gilbert had not yet finished his lecture, but he supplied the last critical facts while he assisted her out of the carriage and ushered her up the steps.

"We shall visit the site of the king's beheading during our next tour of London," he concluded as he opened the door.

"There you are!" Lady Latimer's voice came as a welcome interruption. "We are in here, children. In the library."

Her ladyship and Jeffrey were visible from the vestibule, but Kate did not see the third party till she reached the library entry. A young woman leaning against the mantel—

"Barbara!" Gilbert said warmly. "You have arrived."

"Just a few minutes since," she confirmed. "Which is why I am standing. I've been crammed in a chaise all day, and I doubt I shall ever sit again."

She drew herself up, and Kate entertained an uncharitable suspicion that she often fabricated an excuse to stand because she realized that standing became her. If she were seated, one's attention would focus on the long, narrow face, rendered all the leaner by her enormous coal-colored eyes and thick black hair. But she appeared to be quite tall, though it was difficult to tell without a frame of reference; and so long as she was standing, her face was in proportion to her body. The overall effect was that of a graceful willow—an impression cleverly enhanced by her clinging black carriage dress.

"I have told Barbara all about you"—Lady Latimer beamed from Kate to Miss Dalton and back—"and she's been fairly wild to meet you."

"Miss Dalton," Kate muttered.

"Let us have none of that," her ladyship chided. "Barbara is practically a member of the family. We have known her since she was this high."

Lady Latimer was seated on the mahogany couch, and she indicated a height roughly equal to that of the arms. How long was that? Kate wondered. How old was Miss Dalton? Five-and-twenty at least, she decided, inspecting the long, pale face again. Her father would be growing increasingly anxious to see her wed—

"Must we dwell on the passing years?" Miss Dalton smiled, but her tone was a trifle waspish round the edges. "I have indeed been eager to meet you, Kate. Lord Halstead brought such glowing reports from Bermuda that I was frankly inclined to skepticism. However, I now own that he described you very accurately. Except . . ." She tilted her head and knit her brows. "I expected you to be much taller."

"We have talked about that," Lady Latimer said. "Our conclusion was that Daniel judged Kate to be tall because he himself was so short."

"Then he must have fancied me a giantess," Miss Dalton said dryly.

There was an appreciative titter of laughter; even Kate managed a weak, polite giggle. But she was uncomfortably aware that Miss Dalton's dark eyes were still fastened to the crown of her leghorn hat.

"We have finished our tea," her ladyship said, gesturing to the tray on the sofa table. "But I should be happy to order another pot."

"Not for me." Gilbert shook his head. "I must call on Aunt Agnes before I dress for the evening. I shall see you at Mrs. Newcomb's musicale." He bowed to the three women in turn and retreated into the foyer.

"And you, dear?" Lady Latimer asked as the front door closed behind him. "Would you care for a cup of tea?"

"No, thank you," Kate murmured. "I had tea at Gilbert's, and I should like to rest before the musicale."

"There is ample time for that," her ladyship said. "We are not due at Mrs. Newcomb's till half past eight. Come in and chat a moment."

She patted the place beside her, and Kate stifled a sigh. She had no desire to "chat" with Miss Dalton, but Lady Latimer had destroyed her only credible excuse. She trudged across the room and sank onto the couch.

"I've been most eager to meet you, Kate," Miss Dalton reiterated. "Though I must say I find the situation rather eerie. We have been marveling at the similarity between your background and mine."

"Yes," Kate mumbled. "Jeffrey mentioned that we have a great deal in common."

She glanced at the shield-back chair across the sofa table. Jeffrey was far from showering Miss Dalton with attention, she noted: he was sprawled lazily in the chair, his long legs stretched in front of him and his fingers laced over his ribs. Not that it signified. He had known Miss Dalton since she was *this* high, and he had readily confessed that he was not in love with her.

"So I did." Jeffrey nodded. "But I've subsequently learned of an even more remarkable coincidence. As we were discussing your voyage, we ascertained that Uncle Edwin and Barbara's grandfather sailed from Plymouth on the same ship."

It was fortunate Mr. Sinclair had been such a voluble drunk, Kate reflected, or she would again have been taken by surprise. As it was, she clearly remembered his comment that his parents had set out for America and disembarked in Bermuda instead.

"That is remarkable," she agreed.

"There could not have been many passengers on the *Exeter*," Miss Dalton said. "I daresay Grandpapa and Mr. Sinclair became quite well acquainted."

"I daresay so."

"And I fancy we are lucky to have been born," Miss Dalton added. "In view of the dreadful storm they encountered."

She looked expectantly at Kate, and Kate's stomach once more knotted with panic. It was an all-too-familiar dilemma: whether to pretend to knowledge she didn't have or deny that she ought to have. At length, she chose a middle course.

"Dreadful storm," she echoed noncommittally.

"Perhaps my grandfather exaggerated their peril," Miss Dalton conceded. "Papa always suspected so. But Grandpapa insisted that the ship was in imminent danger of sinking for upward of a week. There was a clergyman aboard —traveling to his new parish in Virginia—and he was praying night and day for divine mercy. Or so Grandpapa said." She chuckled. "What did your grandfather say?"

"He . . . ah . . ." Dear God. Kate had not removed her gloves, and the leather was clinging damply to her palms.

"Kate did not know her grandfather," Lady Latimer said. "Uncle Edwin died long before she was born."

"Yes!" Kate concurred. "That is what I was going to say. That he died long before I was born."

"I am sorry." Miss Dalton shook her head. "Exaggerated or no, the voyage of the *Exeter* was my favorite childhood story. Indeed, it is our favorite family legend. Despite his reservations, Papa relates the tale at every opportunity . . ."

Her voice trailed off, and Kate's eyes flew back to Jeffrey. He was still lounging in the chair, but— another familiar occurrence—his own eyes had narrowed. Was he counting her mistakes? Her gloves were soaked quite through, and she discreetly peeled them off.

"Well," Miss Dalton said brightly, "I fear my journey is starting to tell. I'm still not ready to sit, but I do believe I could lie down for a while."

"Of course, dear." Lady Latimer sketched one of her fond smiles. "Your baggage has been taken to your bedchamber. Will you show Barbara up, Jeffrey? I've put her in the yellow room."

He rose, and when Miss Dalton stepped to his side, Kate observed that she was very tall indeed. The top of her head extended nearly to Jeffrey's nose, and that was without a hat. And without heels, Kate further observed, peering at Miss Dalton's feet: her shoes were flat. Kate's gaze drifted to Miss Dalton's skirt, and her cheeks warmed with irritation. Miss Pryor had assured her that a double row of crepe was the fashionable trimming for a carriage dress, and Miss Dalton's dress had just such a trimming. But there was a circle of Spanish puffs above the hem and a silk rouleau above that and then another row of puffs . . .

The puffs glided out of the room, brushing Jeffrey's white pantaloons, and Kate returned her attention to Lady Latimer. "Is she to stay here indefinitely?" she blurted out.

"The poor child." Her ladyship sighed; obviously—luckily—she had misinterpreted Kate's tone. "As Lady Jersey mentioned, Barbara's mother has been quite ill. She's much improved, I'm happy to say, but she couldn't possibly come to town. In light of our long family friendship, I naturally offered to take Barbara in for the duration of the Season."

"I am sure Miss Dalton is grateful for your kindness," Kate muttered.

"Please do call her Barbara, dear," Lady Latimer reproved gently. "She is sensitive about her father's lack of title, and her feelings are easily wounded. If you persist in being so formal, she might collect that you regard her as your inferior. And nothing could be further from the truth. Indeed, there is every likelihood she will one day be your cousin."

As if on cue, Kate heard a distant peal of laughter—Jeffrey's baritone intermixed with Barbara's merry soprano—and she ground her fingernails into her palms.

"Speaking of Lady Jersey," Lady Latimer continued, "I chanced to encounter her earlier this afternoon. I went out for a bit of shopping, and we met in Leicester Square. She was most impressed with you. She was a trifle miffed that you did not secure permission to waltz, but I reminded her that you are not familiar with our customs."

"Umm," Kate grunted absently. Her ear was still inclined toward the door, but the laughter had died away, and she looked back at Lady Latimer.

"However"—her ladyship emitted an apologetic cough—"Lady Jersey did express some concern about your clothes. She was very gracious about it, of course," she added quickly. "She said she well understood that fashions in the colonies lag behind our own and that it would take you some time to assemble a proper wardrobe."

This did not sound in the least gracious to Kate, but she bit back a sharp retort. She had already recognized that her clothes were out-of-date.

"Fortunately," Lady Latimer went on, "we were near my mantua-maker at the time, and Mrs. Copeland is extremely efficient. So as soon as Lady Jersey proceeded to her milliner, I hurried up the street and consulted with Mrs. Copeland. She promised to finish half a dozen gowns in a week if you could place your order immediately. I therefore took the liberty of scheduling an appointment the first thing tomorrow morning."

Half a dozen gowns? Kate's jaws sagged with dismay. The dresses alone would cost in excess of a hundred pounds, and it would require another hundred for the requisite accessories. But Kitty Sinclair was rich, and Lady Latimer would judge it most peculiar if Kate declined to acquire a "proper wardrobe."

"Very well," she croaked.

"You needn't be alarmed, dear," her ladyship said soothingly. "I shall accompany you to Mrs. Copeland's and be sure she does not take advantage of your inexperience. Come along now. There is still time to rest before Mrs. Newcomb's party."

She stood, and Kate trailed her obediently out of the library and up the staircase. She remembered Jeffrey's remark that one could not escape one's destiny, and she was unable to quell a notion that her destiny was spinning farther and farther beyond her control.

8

"I recommend gold satin for the bodice." Mrs. Copeland laid a swatch of fabric over the drawing in her stylebook. "Gold will complement Miss Sinclair's lovely hair."

"I much prefer blue," Lady Latimer said. She batted Mrs. Copeland's hand away and replaced the gold swatch with one of sapphire. "Kate's eyes are by far her most arresting feature."

"Miss Sinclair's eyes are green as much as blue," the mantua-maker snapped.

"Then a blue-green fabric would be perfect, would it not?" her ladyship snapped back. "Unfortunately, you do not seem to have such a fabric in your inventory. Perhaps we should search among the linen drapers."

"My fabrics are the best in London," Mrs. Copeland said stiffly. "I choose them very carefully."

"But you can choose only a limited number," Lady Latimer pointed out. "A linen draper will naturally have more materials to offer."

"Then let the linen draper make Miss Sinclair's clothes," the seamstress retorted.

They continued to bicker back and forth, and Kate felt a stab of nostalgia for Miss Pryor's tiny, dusty shop in Hamilton. Ordering gowns from Miss Pryor had been a simple matter because her "stylebook" consisted of whatever English magazines had recently come her way. As Lady Jersey had suggested, "recently" was a relative term—the magazines were always months old and sometimes dated back a year or more—but the costume plates looked wonderfully fashionable to the women of Bermuda.

After the client had selected a design that suited her fancy, the choice of a fabric was easier yet: the material was anything the customer could buy, beg, borrow, or steal. In good times, when shipping was unimpeded by war or weather, it would be new fabric purchased from Papa or another local merchant; but in bad times, it could come from almost anywhere. Indeed, two of Kate's "companion" dresses had been made from old draperies she found in Mrs. Todhunter's attic.

At any rate, a visit to Miss Pryor required very few decisions, and Kate was abysmally unprepared to deal with a stylish London seamstress. She should have been warned by the glittering chandeliers and gilt chairs and Aubusson carpets, she reflected, glancing round the shop again. But she had not, and Mrs. Copeland's appearance put her even further at ease. The mantua-maker resembled nothing so much as a kind, rather dowdy grandmother: her plain gray dress precisely matched her hair, and there was a pair of spectacles perched on her nose. After warmly greeting Lady Latimer and her young cousin, she instructed her assistant to record Miss Sinclair's measurements. Meanwhile, she casually added, she would locate "some sketches" Miss Sinclair might wish to consider.

Like the proverbial lamb being led to slaughter, Kate trailed the assistant to one of the fitting

rooms in the rear of the shop. She was gone under
ten minutes, she calculated, but by the time she
returned to the main room, Mrs. Copeland and
Lady Latimer were already engaged in furious
argument. The source of their dispute, Kate saw
with dismay, was "some sketches"—a book
considerably thicker than the Morrow family
Bible. When the mantua-maker beckoned Kate to
the vacant chair between herself and Lady
Latimer and laid the book on her lap, Kate
discovered that it was much heavier than the Bible
as well.

She had been seated in the chair for upward of
two hours now, Kate estimated, while Mrs.
Copeland chattered into one of her ears and Lady
Latimer into the other. The two women could not
seem to agree on anything, and in an effort to keep
both of them reasonably happy, Kate had ordered
far more gowns than she could afford. Or so she
assumed: neither the mantua-maker nor her
ladyship had been sufficiently crass as to mention
the actual price of any garment. But Kate was
grimly certain that a carriage dress, a morning
dress, two walking dresses, and six ball gowns
would reduce her legacy most alarmingly.

"What do you think, dear?" Lady Latimer said.
"The gold or the blue?"

And now they were debating yet another
evening dress. It had to end somewhere, and Kate
firmly shook her head. "I cannot—"

"Cannot decide?" her ladyship interposed. "Then
we shall do one of each. Make the gold corsage plain,
Mrs. Copeland, with a net skirt, and slash the sleeves
of the blue one with lace . . ."

She rattled on, the mantua-maker busily jotting
notes on her order pad, and Kate swallowed her
protest. What were two more gowns when she had
purchased ten already?

"That is it then."

To Kate's immense relief, Mrs. Copeland rose and heaved the stylebook off her lap; apparently even she was satisfied with an order for a full dozen ensembles.

"I promised to complete six gowns by next Friday," the seamstress continued, "and if you will specify which six—"

"Only six?" Lady Latimer essayed a frown of disappointment. "I was in hopes you could finish all twelve. Perhaps we should split the order between you and Madame Girard."

"Umm." Mrs. Copeland pretended to study her order pad. "Maybe I *can* complete all twelve. It will require a great deal of extra work, of course."

"I am sorry to hear that," her ladyship said crisply, "because you will not receive a single extra groat in compensation."

"Then be sure Miss Sinclair comes for her first fitting Tuesday morning," the mantua-maker snapped. "*Early* Tuesday morning," she added with a sniff.

Lady Latimer nodded, stood up, tugged Kate to her feet, and propelled her across the Aubusson carpets to the door. Kate found it peculiarly difficult to walk, and at length, she realized that the weight of the stylebook had rendered her legs quite numb. When they stepped out of the shop, she shook her ladyship's hand from her arm and sagged against the door, waiting for the tingling to subside.

"And now we must search for your accessories," Lady Latimer said brightly. "Since the establishments I patronize are located nearby, I normally go about on foot."

""That would be fine," Kate murmured. "Just

give me a moment to rest." She flexed one leg and then the other, wincing a bit as the blood rushed back.

"Do not be alarmed by my quarrels with Mrs. Copeland." Lady Latimer had obviously misinterpreted the nature of Kate's distress. "We both adore to bargain. I invariably threaten to obtain my fabrics from a linen draper, and she invariably threatens to decline my custom if I do. And neither of us is entirely certain the other wouldn't execute her threat. As a consequence, I purchase all my material from Mrs. Copeland, and she gives me an excellent price."

"I'm sure she does," Kate mumbled. "But . . ." Her voice trailed off.

"But you are concerned that your father might be angry."

Lady Latimer's words were as much a statement as a question, and Kate elected not to respond.

"Which compels me to inquire exactly what arrangements Cousin Robert made." Her ladyship emitted an apologetic little cough. "He must have provided *some* funds to meet your needs before you marry Gilbert."

"I . . . I do have a letter of credit to the Bank of England," Kate stammered.

"Ah." Lady Latimer bobbed her head. "But you fear the money may not be enough. Do not tease yourself about it, dear. When you are as old as I am, you will recognize that no amount of money is *ever* enough, but one somehow makes ends meet. And in your case, rescue is close at hand. I expect Cousin Robert will arrive very shortly."

It was her third or fourth reference to Lord Latimer's imminent arrival, and Kate knit her brows in puzzlement. Mr. Sinclair had clearly stated that his visit to England was unplanned.

"Why do you say that?" she asked aloud.

"Do you not recollect that I wrote to inform him of Daniel's death?"

Kate did vaguely recall her ladyship's reference to such a communication the afternoon they met. "Yes, but—"

"I was not aware at the time that Cousin Robert didn't yet know of Horace's death," Lady Latimer went on, "and I am afraid I was somewhat curt. Well, let me not hide my teeth. The truth is that I ripped your father out a bit. I reminded him that Horace had been gone nearly a year and said I could not but count him rather irresponsible for having neglected his estate so long."

"I see," Kate said, not seeing at all.

"As I told you then, I dispatched the letter early in March. And I am certain that when Cousin Robert received it, he set out for England at once. With fair weather and favorable winds, he should be here any day."

Kate choked down an hysterical giggle. It would take "favorable winds" indeed to blow Lord Latimer back from the dead.

"So you mustn't worry about the cost of your wardrobe," her ladyship concluded. "Are you ready to proceed? We have many merchants left to see."

The feeling had returned to Kate's legs, and she drew herself reluctantly up. Lady Latimer glanced at her landau, which was parked just across the footpath.

"Drake!" she snapped.

The coachman, who had been soundly sleeping on the box, shook himself awake.

"Come along, Drake," her ladyship commanded. "We shall need you to carry our parcels."

In the event, it required more than Drake to accomplish such a monumental task. When they returned to the carriage some three hours later, the coachman was virtually invisible behind a great stack of hatboxes, shoe boxes, and miscellaneous sacks of merchandise, but despite this valiant effort, Kate and Lady Latimer were almost equally burdened. They had traded packages so many times that Kate had long since lost track of who was carrying what, but she believed she had the three shawls, the floral headdress, the parasol, and the muff. (Though she wouldn't need a muff for many months to come, Lady Latimer had counseled her to buy one now while the price of fur was low.) Yes, that was right. Kate had politely insisted that her ladyship take the lighter load—a beaded reticule, two ivory fans, and half a dozen pairs of gloves.

Drake piled the parcels on the rear-facing seat of the landau, handed Kate and Lady Latimer into the seat across, remounted the box, and clucked the horses to a start. Her purchases formed a veritable mountain, Kate observed with horror—extending nearly to the roof of the carriage—and she shuddered to contemplate how much she had spent. Well, not actually *spent*, she amended. Evidently Lady Latimer had excellent credit, for all the merchants had agreed to forward an invoice to Charles Street. But sooner or later, the bills would arrive, and there would be no doting father to pay them.

When they reached the house, her ladyship desired two footmen to assist Drake with the packages, and in the space of a few minutes, the whole great heap had been transferred from the landau to Kate's bed. Though the bed was considerably larger than the carriage seat, the mound of parcels was still a formidable sight, and Kate fancied she would feel better when everything was put away. She removed her hat and gloves, opened the largest of the boxes, plucked out the French bonnet within, and bore it to the wardrobe.

The left-hand door of the wardrobe was ajar, and Kate knit another frown. She had discovered early on that the door was slightly warped—one had to lift it a quarter-inch or so to engage the latch—and she thought she had closed it securely before she left the room. She pulled it on open, opened the right-hand door as well, and frowned again. After Sally had pressed her clothes, Kate had been careful to keep them unwrinkled by distributing the hangers evenly along the rod. Now, she saw, there was a vacant space in the center of the rod, and the garments on either side had been pushed together. The chambermaid had obviously been in the room during Kate's absence—the bed had been made, and there were fresh towels on the rack beside the wash-stand—but the chambermaid had never before moved the contents of the wardrobe.

Kate shoved the bonnet on the wardrobe shelf, hurried to the chest, and opened the top drawer. One of her duties as Mrs. Todhunter's companion had been to keep the old widow's clothes in order, and one of Mrs. Todhunter's many eccentricities had been an obsession for neatness in the arrangement of her underthings. Eventually, by force of habit, Kate had become a stickler for neatness herself, and she perceived at once that her own undergarments had been disturbed. Only a little— so little that a less critical eye would not have noticed. But the uppermost of her corsets was a trifle askew, overlapping the adjacent stack of stockings.

A thief? Kate wondered wildly. She dashed to the dressing table and raised the lid of her jewelry box. In addition to the pearls, Mrs. Todhunter had willed her a ruby-and-diamond brooch and matching earrings, and none of the pieces was missing. Not a thief then. Which could only mean . . .

Kate's mouth went dry, and she raced back to the wardrobe. Her pelisse was hanging on the far left side, and she jerked it out and plunged her hand through the long tear in the satin lining. The documents Mr. Cottle had supplied her were the only proof of her true identity, and she had judged this the ideal place to hide them: behind the tattered lining of her ancient cloak. Her fingers encountered paper, and with a sigh of relief, she withdrew two familiar ivory envelopes. One was her letter of credit, directed to the Bank of England, and the other was a letter of introduction to a London solicitor. (In the remote event she should require legal assistance, Mr. Cottle had said.) The seals of both envelopes remained unbroken, and Kate counted it safe to assume they had not been found.

But that was scant comfort, she reflected grimly, dropping the envelopes back through the slit. It was clear that someone suspected her imposture and had searched her room in hopes of locating some supporting evidence. Lady Latimer had been away from home all day, and Gilbert was far too unimaginative to admit himself to the house, creep up two flights of stairs, and rummage round her bedchamber. And that, of course, left—

"Ah, you are back."

"Jeffrey!" Kate whirled toward the door, instinctively clutching the pelisse to her chest.

"Is something amiss?"

His eyes widened with every indication of concern, and Kate hesitated. Was he trying to ascertain whether she had noticed his search? She was tempted to enumerate the several things that were, indeed, "amiss" and gauge his reaction, but she realized that she might have leapt to a premature conclusion. Perhaps Lady Latimer had instructed Sally to check the condition of Miss Sinclair's clothes. In either case, any mention of a search would be disastrous: serving to persuade Jeffrey—or confirm his opinion—that there was something worth searching for.

"N-no," she stuttered. "You merely startled me."

"I am sorry for that." He stepped over the threshold and crossed to her side. "Do you find our English weather so chilly?" he said, frowning at her cloak.

Kate started to reply that she did, then recollected that the weather today was pleasantly warm even by Bermudian standards. "N-no," she stammered again. "I wanted to determine if my . . . my new bonnet matched my pelisse."

In fact, none of the hats she had purchased remotely resembled the slate-gray cloak, and she held her breath for fear he would demand to see the mythical new bonnet for himself. But he nodded, and she hastily returned the pelisse to the wardrobe.

"It appears your shopping excursion was quite successful." Jeffrey shifted his eyes to the bed. "You are accumulating an extensive trousseau."

Kate wondered what would happen if she blurted out that there was no trousseau—that she was not Kitty Sinclair and had no intention of wedding Gilbert. But she had resolved to think before she spoke, and she said nothing.

"However, I did not come to talk about your clothes." Jeffrey cleared his throat and looked back at her. "I wanted to clarify the remarks I made at Almack's."

Kate's heart crashed against her ribs. Evidently he had decided not to marry Miss Dalton—

"In retrospect," he went on, "I recognize that I must have sounded rather . . . rather ghoulish. It no doubt appeared that I am eagerly awaiting Cousin Robert's death, and nothing could be further from the truth. I can live indefinitely on my present income, and I daresay I could live forever without a title."

He flashed a wry grin, then sobered. "At any rate, I sincerely hope your father is blessed with many happy, healthy years in future. And I apologize if my comments implied otherwise."

"That is all right," Kate said stiffly. She was literally frozen with disappointment; she could scarcely move her lips.

"Well!"

Jeffrey rubbed his palms together, shuffled his feet, brushed an imaginary speck of lint from his coat. He did not seem to know what to say next, and Kate wished he would admit defeat and go.

"Well," he resumed at last. "Did you enjoy your outing with Gilbert? I've had no chance to ask."

"Our tour was most instructive," she muttered.

"You are finding yourselves compatible, I trust? Gilbert and I have been friends since infancy, and I can't judge him objectively. But I believe he is generally regarded as a pleasant fellow."

"Yes," Kate agreed. "He is very pleasant."

And that exhausted the subject of Gilbert, she thought. Like his physical features, his character was colorless—his virtues and faults tending to run together. There was another interval of silence, and she became aware that Jeffrey's eyes were resting expectantly on her face. Apparently courtesy dictated that she compliment his *parti* in turn.

"As is Miss Dalton," she added. "I've had no chance to mention that either. She seems extremely . . . pleasant."

"Yes." His tone was peculiarly hollow, as if Kate had somehow failed to fulfill his expectations. "As I indicated at Almack's, we get on well enough." He lowered his eyes and turned away.

"Then you should be quite happy together," Kate snapped. "You also indicated that *getting on* is the best one can hope of marriage." She had already said too much, but the lingering, aching disappointment drove her on. "Has it never occurred to you that love might exist after all?"

She stopped and clenched her hands, appalled that she had made such a dreadful cake of herself. He would laugh now, she fancied, or offer some derisive rejoinder. But when he spun back round, she saw that his eyes had narrowed to golden slits of anger.

"You're a fine one to prate of love," he hissed. "At least, I know Barbara; I was acquainted with her for many years before there was any talk of marriage. You came thousands of miles across the sea to wed a man you'd yet to meet."

Kate instinctively opened her mouth to protest, then realized there was nothing she could say: if she denied his charge, she would be compelled to reveal her impersonation. She closed her mouth and bit her lip.

"And I, at least, am honest," Jeffrey continued, still in a savage whisper. "I am fond of Barbara, and I enjoy her company, and I claim no deeper feelings. But that is not enough for you, is it? No, you will not be content until you persuade yourself that you are wildly in love with Gilbert. That is the only way you can justify the marriage, is it not?"

"No!" Kate croaked. "I—"

"Forgive me."

He waved her to silence, and the motion appeared to dispel his anger as well. He dropped his hand, and when he went on, his voice was normal.

"I have no right to judge you. But you haven't the right to judge me either; that was my point. Which brings us back to your original question."

"It isn't important," Kate mumbled.

"Yes, it is," he said quietly. "It is excessively important. It *has* occurred to me that love may exist. I have been pondering that possibility since . . ." He hesitated. "Since our discussion at Almack's."

His eyes darkened, and he raised his hand again—slowly and awkwardly, like the hand of a marionette. It stopped mere inches from Kate's face, and she thought for one breathtaking instant that he was going to touch her. But his arm jerked backward instead, and he fumbled with the stiff, snowy folds of his neckcloth.

"It has occurred to me," he repeated. "But there is also the matter of honor, Kate."

Another silence; Kate could hear the rhythmic tick of the mantel clock and the twittering of a bird beyond the window. Then Jeffrey looked away, and the spell was broken.

"Well," he said again, "I shall leave you to unpack your treasures in peace. Cousin Jane will insist we depart for the opera at precisely half past seven. I shall see you then."

He bowed and strode back across the room, and Kate's heart began to race again. Honor! She had considered this complication, she recalled; indeed, she had started to explain to Jeffrey that her engagement was tentative. But Lady Latimer had interrupted, and Kate had not perceived that the complication was a fatal one. Not until now. Jeffrey had all but said that he could never undertake to court her so long as she was committed to Gilbert—his friend "since infancy."

Kate was inclined to rush after him and confess her masquerade at once, but she feared such a course might do more harm than good. Though Jeffrey had obliquely professed his attraction as well, she needed time to gain his trust before she admitted her deception. It therefore seemed best to adhere to her original plan: she would "receive" the news of her father's death, her engagement to Gilbert would be terminated, and she could then set about to win Jeffrey's affection. And if the letter from Mr. Wilcox was "delivered" in tomorrow's post, the delay would be less than four-and-twenty hours.

Kate hurried to the *bonheur-du-jour* desk beneath the window. The inkstand was full, she saw, removing the pen to check, and when she opened the center drawer, she found an ample supply of plain stationery. She sank into the chair, plucked the top sheet of paper from the drawer, and snatched up the pen.

"March 31, 1816," she scrawled at the top of the page. That, she remembered, was the date Mr. Wilcox should have returned to St. George's. "My dear Kate . . ."

She leaned back in the chair to compose an introductory sentence and belatedly recollected that she still did not know whether Jeffrey had searched her room. But it didn't signify, she decided. When she sadly announced that Mr. Sinclair was the *late* Lord Latimer, the situation would be altogether different. She sat forward and dipped the pen in the inkstand again.

"It is with heavy heart that I must inform you . . ."

9

Kate crumpled the final rough draft of her letter and dropped it in the lining of her pelisse. She fervently hoped the weather would not turn cold, for her cloak was fairly stuffed by now with the multitudinous wads of paper she had discarded during the past three days.

She had completed the initial draft quite easily and secreted it in the pelisse before she dressed for the opera Friday evening. But when she reviewed the letter Saturday morning, prior to "finding" it in the post, she observed a host of flaws. The date, to begin with. Her voyage to England had been plagued by an abnormal series of problems, and it seemed unlikely that the next ship would meet with equal ill fortune. She changed the date to April 10 and hastily recopied the rest of the letter.

But what of the salutation? she wondered, rereading the second draft. The late Lord Latimer had called his daughter Kitty; would Mr. Wilcox not use the same name? He and Mr. Sinclair had formed their partnership long before Kitty was born, and old habits were hard to break. Which also shed suspicion on the body of the letter. "It is with heavy heart that I must inform you . . ." No, Kate realized, she had once more confused her background with Kitty's. The words she had composed were those of a stranger, and Mr. Wilcox had known Kitty Sinclair all her life.

In short, the letter would have to be entirely rewritten, and it was too late to finish before the mail arrived. Indeed, it was too late even to *start*: the Latimer household had been invited to a breakfast party at General Waller's. Kate slipped both drafts behind the lining of her cloak and decided to begin anew on Sunday, when her mind was fresh.

However, Sunday proved to be a very bad day for such an endeavor. Lady Latimer insisted they all attend services at St. George's, Hanover Square, and as luck would have it, the subject of the sermon was Dishonesty. The rector's stern admonitions not to steal or bear false witness against one's neighbor were still ringing in Kate's ears when she finished dinner and repaired to her bedchamber, and each new draft of her letter seemed more Dishonest than the last. After eight or ten abortive efforts, she had resigned herself to missing Monday's post as well and started all over this morning.

And at last, or so she believed, she had produced a satisfactory communication. She had virtually memorized the letter by now, but she reviewed it once more to be certain there was nothing she had overlooked. "My dearest Catherine," it began. This, she fancied, neatly avoided the question of which nickname Mr. Wilcox would use and simultaneously injected a note of warmth. "My deepest wish is that I could personally convey the sad news I am compelled to report."

Yes, she thought, that was much better. She read on, nodding with approval from time to time. It had occurred to her that some person of authority in Bermuda—the vicar of St. Peter's, even the governor—might eventually notify Mr. Sinclair's English relatives of his death. She had consequently sought a middle course in the matter of dates as well, stating that though "your dear father" had died "soon after your departure," Mr.

Wilcox had been "so occupied" by the funeral arrangements and subsequent press of business that he had been unable to write "for some days thereafter." Lest this sound too brusque, Kate had added another warm touch: an emotional description of the funeral. She would be pleased to learn, the letter concluded, that "the church was overflowing with Robert's many friends and professional associates."

That was *very* good, Kate judged; it actually brought a small lump to her throat. There remained only to write an envelope, and she glanced at the mantel clock. The envelope would have to wait, she saw; it was half past six, and she had not yet dressed for dinner. She patted her cloak as smooth as she could, carefully inserted the letter through the slit in the lining, and rang for Sally.

Gilbert's Aunt Agnes was engaged to dine with them, Kate remembered as she descended the stairs, but when she reached the vestibule, the earl was advising Lady Latimer that his elderly aunt was ill. Fortunately, the illness was not a serious one—merely a nasty spring cold. Not serious *now*, he amended darkly: at Aunt Agnes's advanced age, any malady could ultimately prove fatal.

Malady! Kate thought. Her letter failed to specify the cause of Mr. Sinclair's death. But surely it was clear from the context that he had suffered some sort of sudden attack.

"How true." Lady Latimer sadly shook her head. "As I grow older, I find it increasingly difficult to recover from even the mildest complaints. Indeed, though I didn't wish to mention it, I fear I am coming down with a cold myself. I pray I shan't be too sick to attend my own assembly."

Her ladyship *was* sniffling a bit, Kate noticed as they trooped to the dining room and were seated

round the table. However, her incipient cold did
not appear to have affected her tongue, for as soon
as the soup was served, she began to chatter of her
preparations for the ball. Kate felt a prickle of
guilt. Even if she succeeded in persuading Lady
Latimer to proceed with the assembly, the news of
Cousin Robert's death would inevitably cloud the
festivities. But that could not be helped. Jeffrey
had unmistakably implied that her engagement to
Gilbert was the only obstacle between them, and it
was therefore imperative to terminate the engagement at once.

The earl was seated in the chair next to hers,
and Kate cast him a sideward glance from beneath
her lashes. How would he react to the news? she
wondered. He had already calculated, farthing by
farthing, exactly how he would spend Kitty
Sinclair's dowry. But she need entertain no guilt
on that head, Kate decided. Kitty would not have
wed Gilbert in any case; she had eloped with her
American suitor while her father was still alive.

And Gilbert was unlikely to die of heartbreak,
Kate reflected wryly, gazing back at her soup. She
had never had a *parti*, but it required no
experience to recognize that the earl's attentions
were desultory in the extreme. He had dutifully
introduced her to a few of his friends at the
musicale and the opera and General Waller's
breakfast, but they had had no private conversation on any of those occasions. Nor at any
other time: following their tour of London, Gilbert
had not called during the day.

So she needn't tease herself about the earl's
feelings either, Kate concluded. He would be
disappointed to lose her dowry, but now he had a
title, he would readily find another woman of
fortune to marry. Lady Latimer cleared her

throat, and Kate became aware that she was the only person who had not yet finished her soup. She hastily gulped it down and replaced the spoon on her plate.

Her ladyship signaled for the soup bowls to be removed, and as the footmen stepped forward, the peal of the doorbell echoed through the dining room.

"What a peculiar time to be calling!" Lady Latimer emitted a sniff of vexation. "Tell whoever it is that we are at dinner, Adams, and cannot be disturbed."

The butler strode obediently into the vestibule, and her ladyship frowned down the table at Gilbert.

"Could it be Agnes, dear? Perhaps she decided she was well enough to join us after all."

"I think not." The earl shook his head. "Aunt Agnes's abigail was bringing her dinner to her bed-chamber just as I departed."

Kate heard the creak of the front door, an indecipherable murmur of voices, and then the rapid tap of footfalls on the foyer floor.

"Lady Latimer!" Adams ground to a halt in the archway. "Begging your pardon, ma'am, but I felt sure you would wish to receive this caller." He wrung his hands with excitement. "It is your cousin, ma'am! Miss Sinclair's father! Lord Latimer has come from Bermuda!"

Kate sat silently, motionlessly, paralyzed with shock. She fancied that a very long time elapsed, that everyone must be staring at her. But when she regained sufficient sense to move her eyes, she realized that only a few seconds could have passed. Lady Latimer was just assuming one of her bright smiles, and Jeffrey and Miss Dalton were turning their heads toward the archway.

"How wonderful!" Her ladyship clapped her own hands. "Do show him in, Adams."

What had happened? Kate thought wildly as the butler returned to the foyer. Well, it was obvious what had happened: Mr. Sinclair hadn't died after all. Mr. Barnes's chambermaid was not a qualified medical authority, and she had apparently mistaken a deep sleep for the final sleep of death. In fact, Mr. Sinclair had probably been in some sort of coma. Evidently it had taken him several weeks to recover, and when he had, he had resumed his interrupted journey.

"Lord Latimer," Adams announced grandly, reappearing in the archway.

He stepped aside, and Kate froze with shock again, for the man looming up behind him was not Mr. Sinclair. He was approximately Mr. Sinclair's age, she judged—in his early sixties—and he did bear a superficial resemblance to the late Lord Latimer. He, too, was a large man, though neither so tall nor so heavy as Mr. Sinclair, and he possessed a similar thatch of thick gray hair. But Kate clearly remembered Mr. Sinclair's enormous, almost-black eyes, and this man's eyes were small and a frosty gray in hue.

"Cousin Robert!" Lady Latimer leapt to her feet and bounded forward to greet him.

"Cousin Jane. What a pleasure it is to meet you after all these years." He executed a gallant bow, straightened, and turned to Jeffrey. "And you are Jeffrey, of course." He extended his right hand. "You bear a keen likeness to your father."

"So I have been told." Jeffrey rose and shook the proffered hand.

"And this is a dear friend of the family," Lady Latimer said. "Miss Barbara Dalton."

"Miss Dalton." The alleged Lord Latimer bowed to her, then transferred his eyes across the table. "And you must be Gilbert. You look a great deal like your father as well."

"Yes, sir."

The earl also tried to stand, but one leg of his chair caught in the carpet, and the footmen—absorbed in the drama of the moment—failed to notice his plight. As a consequence, he was trapped in an awkward half-crouch, his thighs jammed against the edge of the table.

"I was immensely sorry to learn of Daniel's death." The caller sorrowfully shook his head. "Though we were acquainted only briefly, I grew quite fond of him."

"Thank you, sir."

"And that leaves you, my dear." The man shifted his gaze abruptly to Kate. "Has the cat seized your tongue?"

"I . . ." She licked her lips. "I—"

"You are astonished that I am here," he interposed. "Which is quite understandable in the circumstances. Forgive me, Cousin Jane." He swung his eyes back to Lady Latimer. "I did not know of Cousin Horace's passing until I received your recent letter. Had I known, I should naturally have come to England long since. I trust you will accept my belated condolences."

"And I trust you will accept my apologies," her ladyship murmured. "I was much too harsh, I fear, but I did not comprehend the situation when I wrote. After I discussed the matter with Kate, I surmised that the letter from Horace's solicitor had gone astray."

"It must have." The visitor heaved a regretful sigh. "You may or may not be aware that there is no organized postal system in Bermuda. We pray that communications from abroad will be delivered to the proper party, but unfortunately, many messages are lost."—

"I wasn't aware of that," Lady Latimer said, "but I am not surprised. Horace always felt that Bermuda was a most uncivilized place."

"How right he was. Now, if you will pardon me again, I should like a private word with my daughter."

"Of course you would." Her ladyship beamed from him to Kate. "The library would be most convenient. Kate knows where it is."

Gilbert had extricated himself from his chair by now, and he assisted Kate to her feet. She was sure she would stumble and fall before she could make her way around the table, but by some miracle, she reached the archway more or less intact. The stranger politely nodded her ahead of him, and she led him across the entry hall and through the door on the opposite side.

"You are not Lord Latimer," she blurted out when he had closed the door behind them.

"And you are not Kitty Sinclair," he countered. "You have persuaded them that you are Kitty"— he waved toward the dining room—"but you are actually Catherine Morrow."

Kate's mouth fell open, and he chuckled.

"My dear child." He shook his head again. "I was plotting and scheming before you were a gleam in your father's eye. When Lady Latimer's butler remarked that my daughter would be delighted to see me, I knew he couldn't be referring to Kitty. Not the real Kitty; she is in Virginia. And the only person with the opportunity to pose as Kitty was the young woman who so eloquently advised me of Robert's death."

"Then you are Mr. Wilcox," Kate said gratuitously.

"Yes. Though I strongly suggest you develop the habit of addressing me as Papa. I collect that you prefer to be called Kate?" She nodded. "And how did you explain that discrepancy to Lady Latimer?"

"As it happens, I was called Kitty as a child . . ." She briefly related the initial confusion surrounding her nickname and the conclusion her ladyship had drawn.

"How convenient," Mr. Wilcox said. "Should I err and refer to you as Kitty, no question will be raised."

"No!" Kate protested. "You don't understand—"

"I understand very well," he interrupted. "Barnes mentioned that Robert was quite foxed the night he died. Which was not an unusual occurrence, I am sorry to say. I expect he babbled out the whole history of his life, including a report of Kitty's elopement. At least, I presume she eloped. I did not know she had gone to Virginia until I read your letter. I then recalled that Robert —over another heavy wet—complained of her friendship with an American sea captain."

"Yes, but—"

"The next morning," he went on, "you learned of Robert's death and decided to represent yourself as his daughter. It was a pleasant bonus when you reached England and further discovered that your adopted father had become a viscount."

"Yes, but I didn't *plan*—"

"My situation is similar." Mr. Wilcox once more cut her off. "A few days after my return to St. George's, Lady Latimer's letter was delivered to our office, and I, too, glimpsed a golden opportunity. I was aware that Robert had never met his English relatives. Except for Jeffrey's father, and I knew he had died long since. Lord Halstead was the only person who could identify Robert, and suddenly . . ." He snapped his fingers. "Suddenly, Lord Halstead was gone. I calculated that I could readily take Robert's place. I always did fancy the notion of being a peer."

He smiled and patted Kate's shoulder. "And if we cooperate, we can both attain our objectives. I can be Viscount Latimer, and you can be the Countess of Halstead."

"No!" Kate repeated. "I have no wish to marry Gilbert. And even if I did, there is a grave complication. Mr. Sinclair pledged Lord Halstead a substantial dowry."

"So he told me. Fifteen thousand pounds, I believe he said." Mr. Wilcox's tone was wonderfully casual. "I assure you that presents no problem. I am an excessively wealthy man—doubly so now Robert is dead. I have invested fifteen thousand pounds in far riskier enterprises than this. I fully anticipate that I shall recoup all my money the first year and earn a profit every year thereafter."

He gazed proprietarily around the library, and Kate wondered whether she should tell him that the town house was not a part of the entailed property. Before she could decide, he strode to the liquor cabinet beside the fireplace and poured himself a generous glass of brandy.

"Though I hope to persuade young Halstead to accept somewhat less," he added, turning back to face her. "However safe the project, it is foolish to invest more than one must."

Kate belatedly perceived that she should never have mentioned the dowry; she had merely postponed—and clouded—the real issue. "There is another complication," she rejoined aloud. "One I did not recognize till after I arrived. Were it not for Mr. Sinclair, Jeffrey would inherit Lord Latimer's estate."

Which Lord Latimer? By her count, there were now four to choose from. She repressed an hysterical inclination to giggle. "Cousin Horace's estate," she elaborated.

"So he would. But what has that to do with us?" Mr. Wilcox looked genuinely puzzled, and Kate's mirth evaporated.

"I shan't be a party to defrauding Jeffrey," she said firmly. "No permanent harm has yet been done, and I have devised a way to ensure that he will receive his inheritance at once. I . . ."

Her voice trailed off. She had been at the point of describing the letter she had so painstakingly composed, but that would be another mistake. The letter was useless now: it purported to come from Mr. Wilcox, and Mr. Wilcox was here. As he himself had stated, it was foolish to risk more than one must. There was no reason to reveal that she had concocted a second deception on top of the first.

"I intend to tell Jeffrey the truth at the earliest opportunity," she finished lamely.

"No, you will not." Mr. Wilcox's amiability vanished; his eyes were as cold and forbidding as a gray winter sky. "I did not travel all the way across the sea to have my plans thwarted by a green-headed chit of a girl."

"I can well conceive your disappointment," Kate said as politely as she could. "But"—she elected to borrow from Jeffrey—"there is the matter of honor."

"Honor?" Mr. Wilcox laughed, but the sound was devoid of amusement. "That's a fine word to come from you. Barnes advised me of your background as well. You inveigled a considerable sum of money from your late employer, did you not?"

"No, I did not." Kate struggled to maintain a calm, courteous tone; it wouldn't do to lose her temper. "But that is neither here nor there. I won't abet any scheme to steal Jeffrey's legacy."

"A noble sentiment." Mr. Wilcox swirled the brandy round his glass. "Though somewhat tardy, I fear." He took a sip of the brandy and smacked his lips with appreciation. "The fact is that at this juncture, you have no choice but to cast your lot with mine."

"No choice?" Kate echoed.

"Think it through, my dear." He sounded almost kind again. "I am claiming to be Lord Latimer, and you are claiming to be Kitty Sinclair. If we mutually accuse one another of deceit, it will be left to them to render judgment." He gestured once more toward the dining room. "Robert and I were partners for thirty years. I have known Kitty all her life. I met and conversed with Lord Halstead. You based your entire impersonation on a few scraps of drunken conversation. Who would be the more credible?"

It was clearly a rhetorical question, and Kate elected not to respond.

"At the very least," Mr. Wilcox continued, "you would be evicted from the house and banned from society. At worst, the Sinclairs might also initiate legal proceedings against you."

He was right, Kate owned, but she sensed a flaw in his logic. She frowned, reviewing their discussion, and at length, it came to her.

"Then why do you not expose me anyway?" she demanded. "Why invest even a groat when you've only to tell them I am not Kitty Sinclair?"

"Because I judge it best not to create an

atmosphere of suspicion. You have obviously played your part very cleverly, and if you are revealed to be an impostor, it might occur to them to question my identity as well."

"No," Kate said triumphantly, remembering the conversation in the dining room. "You cannot expose me because you have already acknowledged me to be your daughter."

"That was an error," he conceded. "However, I fancy I could explain myself to their satisfaction. I could state that you are a young woman I once employed. A"—he paused for dramatic emphasis —"a mentally unbalanced young woman who frequently suffers from the delusion that she is Kitty Sinclair. I decided to speak with you privately in hopes of dispelling this insane notion, but unfortunately, I was unable to do so. To the contrary, you have now conceived the further delusion that I am not Kitty's father."

Was it possible? Kate wondered wildly. Could he actually persuade Lady Latimer and Jeffrey and Gilbert that she was mad?

"It would not be easy." Mr. Wilcox might have been reading her mind. "But when we begin to compare notes of names and dates and events . . ." His voice trailed provocatively off. "I do believe I should win, and you would be wise to consider the ramifications of my victory. There might be general—albeit regretful—agreement that you should be confined in Bedlam until you regain your faculties."

Bedlam! Kate shuddered. Though the infamous asylum had recently been moved to a new building, it remained infinitely worse than any prison.

"You really have no choice," Mr. Wilcox reiterated, resuming his kind tone. "And if you can overcome your moral indignation for a moment, you will realize that I am asking very little. You need only continue the impersonation you yourself devised. I shan't even insist you marry Gilbert. Indeed, should you reject him, I shall tender the appropriate apologies."

He took another sip of brandy, but Kate had been stricken dumb again.

"However, if you will allow me a bit of fatherly advice, I must strongly recommend you do wed Gilbert." Mr. Wilcox attempted—unsuccessfully— a fond, paternal smile. "You are unlikely to make a better match, and I may not be so generous with the next *parti* who happens along."

"No!" Kate found her tongue. "I told you at the outset—"

"Do not be overly hasty, dear." Mr. Wilcox waved her to silence. "Robert and I accumulated half a million pounds between us, and much of our prosperity was due to a very simple strategy. We never acted rashly; we delayed every decision till the last, critical instant. I shall start negotiating the details of your dowry with young Halstead. Should the necessity arise, I can always announce that you have changed your mind."

He drained the rest of his brandy and set the empty glass on the liquor cabinet. "Are you ready then? We mustn't be absent too long."

In point of fact, Kate was not ready, but she had no choice on this head either: Mr. Wilcox strode forward, took her arm, and ushered her out of the library and back across the vestibule.

"There you are!" Lady Latimer said gaily. "I desired the entrée to be held. I presume you have not eaten, Cousin Robert? Luckily, Gilbert's Aunt Agnes is indisposed this evening. Well, not luckily for *her*, of course," she amended. "But there is a surplus of food, and Agnes's place had already been laid."

She indicated the vacant chair at the foot of the table, and as Adams escorted Kate to her own place, Mr. Wilcox sat down.

"I trust your voyage was a smooth one?" Her ladyship rattled on. "Poor Kate was en route above six weeks and seasick much of that."

Not half so sick as she was now, Kate reflected miserably. The footmen presented the main course, and her stomach churned at the sight of the pigeon pie, creamed potatoes, and French beans. She feared her distress must be clearly written on her face, and she glanced apprehensively round the table. But no one was attending her, she saw with relief; they were all looking at Mr. Wilcox and listening to his account of his journey. Jeffrey appeared particularly enthralled, his amber eyes narrowed in concentration—

There was a burst of appreciative laughter; evidently Mr. Wilcox had concluded his narrative with a witticism.

"At least, you experienced none of the problems our ancestors encountered when they sailed *to* the New World," Miss Dalton said. "Jeffrey and I realized just a few days since that your parents and my grandfather were together on the *Exeter*. Grandpapa went on to America."

"That was most courageous of him in the circumstances," Mr. Wilcox said wryly. "My parents were bound for Virginia as well, but they had had quite enough of seafaring by the time they reached Bermuda. As you probably know, Miss Dalton, there were thirteen passengers on the *Exeter*, and they soon came to judge that an excessively unfavorable number indeed. I am given to understand that when the ship docked at St. George's, they all rushed down the plank, dropped to their knees, and kissed the sand."

"So they they did!" Miss Dalton clapped her hands. "In fact, Grandpapa put some sand in a little bag and carried it with him to America. He later had the sand encased in a locket, and my grandmother willed the locket to me. I regard it as a lucky talisman and take it with me wherever I go."

"And has it brought you luck, my dear?"

"That remains to be seen."

Miss Dalton darted a coquettish look at Jeffrey, but he was still studying Mr. Wilcox.

"Unfortunately, our family has no souvenir of the voyage," Mr. Wilcox said. "But with or without a locket, the journey of the *Exeter* is a highly entertaining story."

"Highly," Jeffrey agreed. "That is why I could scarcely believe that Kate had never heard it."

"She certainly would have heard it had Papa lived to tell her the tale." Mr. Wilcox chuckled. "In my childhood, I welcomed the advent of a storm because he would relate the story again as soon as the wind started howling round the windows. But he died long before Kate was born."

Mr. Wilcox sighed with regret and took a delicate sip of his wine. "And I didn't wish to alarm her. My business requires frequent sea travel, and I did not want poor Kate to fear I should be lost in a shipwreck each time I ventured out of port."

"You were very wise in that respect," Lady Latimer murmured.

And very clever in every respect, Kate thought grimly. Were she suddenly to announce that he was an impostor, the rest of the party would conclude that she was, indeed, quite mad. As Mr. Wilcox had pointed out, he had the advantage of thirty years' acquaintance with Mr. Sinclair. He had heard his partner's stories so often that the details were etched in his memory—as easily recalled as the details of his own life. And where memory wouldn't serve, Mr. Wilcox's devious mind and glib tongue could readily fabricate a credible explanation of events.

"Umm." Jeffrey issued a noncommittal grunt. "I was even more astonished to learn that you hadn't told Kate of Papa's visit to Bermuda. Of your attack on the American warship, I mean. That was *my* favorite childhood tale."

"But you were a boy," Mr. Wilcox said smoothly. "It is one thing to discuss one's youthful indiscretions with a son and quite another to disclose them to a daughter. A daughter may conceive the misguided notion that there is no danger in wedding a wild, irresponsible young man. Forgetting that some men mature with age while others . . ." He stopped and sipped his wine again. "Others merely age."

He was unmistakably referring to Alfred Sinclair, and Jeffrey flushed and peered into his own wineglass. There was a moment of awkward silence—a moment stretching toward infinity—before Lady Latimer pounded to the rescue.

"Well!" her ladyship said brightly. "I am grateful you came so soon after receiving my letter. Though I shan't profess to be surprised. I assured Kate you would be here in ample time to pay for her clothes. Did I not, my dear?" she beamed at Kate."

"Yes," Kate muttered.

"And you are not to be angry with her, Cousin Robert," Lady Latimer added severely, transferring her attention back to Mr. Wilcox. "If you choose to be vexed, be vexed with me. I fairly *forced* Kate to order a dozen new gowns from my mantua-maker. Which reminds me . . ."

She shifted her eyes to Kate again; the interchange was beginning to resemble a tennis match.

"You are scheduled to return for your first fitting tomorrow morning, and I fancy we should go back to the milliner as well. The more I think on it, the more I am persuaded that we can have the Kent toque you admired for *much* less than they are asking. And now your father is here to settle your accounts, you needn't tease yourself about a pound or two."

"Women!" Mr. Wilcox shook his head with mock exasperation. "That is another problem with daughters. Women have no respect for money. A woman will purchase a new gown before she has a roof over her head or food in the larder. Always assuming that a doting father or brother or husband will pay the bills when they arrive. And to the eternal detriment of the male sex, the men invariably open their purses. Pray that you and Kate are blessed with no female children, Gilbert."

He sketched a jovial grin, but the smile didn't reach his cold gray eyes. His eyes, when they darted to Kate, proposed an addendum to their bargain. If she sustained their mutual charade, he would settle her debts. If she betrayed him, she might escape Newgate or Bedlam, but she would ultimately starve in the streets.

"I shall keep that in mind, sir," the earl said politely. "For the present, however, I must beg to be excused." He laid his napkin on the table and rose. "As Aunt Jane mentioned, my Aunt Agnes is indisposed. She's well advanced in years—Aunt Agnes, that is—and I should like to ascertain her condition before her servants retire for the night."

"No apology is necessary." Mr. Wilcox stood as well. "I am beginning to feel the effects of my journey, and I daresay I should retire myself.

Perhaps you could drive me to a convenient hotel."

"Hotel!" Lady Latimer echoed indignantly. "What nonsense! One of the guest bedchambers is vacant, and I *insist* you use it. I shall take you up at once."

"How good of you, Cousin Jane."

Mr. Wilcox heaved a dramatic sigh of gratitude and strode around the table, pausing behind Miss Dalton's chair to pat her shoulder.

"I am eager to see your locket," he said. "Lucky or no, it is a most unusual memento."

"Then I shall show it to you now." Miss Dalton smiled up at him. "I wore it this afternoon, and it's still at the top of my jewelry box."

She seemed to imply that if it fell to the bottom of the box, it might be lost forever. Buried beneath heaps and heaps of priceless gems . . . But she was being unfair, Kate conceded. It was not Miss Dalton's fault that her jewels alone were immensely more valuable than Kate's entire legacy—

Her legacy! Kate was struck by a new and terrible fear. Mr. Wilcox had obviously investigated her background. He would have learned about her letter of credit, and a man of his wealth and influence undoubtedly had contacts at the Bank of England. If she defied him, he could probably arrange to have her funds withheld, and she would starve in the streets indeed—

"Good night, my dear."

Mr. Wilcox interrupted Kate's dark speculation, and she started and looked up at him. His eyes were glittering with triumph, as though he had been reading her mind. You have no choice, the eyes reminded her. I hold all the cards, and I shall inevitably win.

"Good . . . good night," she stammered.

Gilbert and Lady Latimer had reached the archway by now, and Mr. Wilcox gallantly assisted Miss Dalton out of her chair. The four of them trooped into the vestibule, everyone chattering at once, but at length, the earl's voice rose above the rest. He really must leave, Gilbert said, but he would like to call on Lord Latimer tomorrow. Apparently "Lord Latimer" concurred in this proposal, for a few seconds later, the front door slammed closed. The chatter—slightly reduced in volume by Gilbert's departure—drifted up the staircase, diminished to a distant buzz, then faded altogether.

Kate glanced nervously round the dining room, but she and Jeffrey were quite alone; the servants had been dismissed immediately after they served dessert. She gazed into her blancmange, bitterly regretting that she had lacked the wit to excuse herself when the others did. There was nothing for it now but to eat the pudding, which had degenerated to a thick, curdled puddle.

"I'm certain you were delighted by your father's safe arrival," Jeffrey said.

Kate raised her eyes, prepared to mumble that she was, but his appearance shocked her to silence. *Mottled*, she thought, recollecting a descriptive passage from some otherwise-forgotten novel; his complexion was mottled with emotion. His flush had receded, leaving two crimson slashes high on either cheek, and there were white grooves of fury at the corners of his mouth.

"Delighted and relieved." Jeffrey shoved his own pudding savagely away, and the bowl tipped over, spilling a pool of blancmange on the lace tablecloth. "It must have been exceedingly difficult to undertake such a monumental project alone. I am compelled to grant you credit for that."

Project? Kate's head whirled with confusion. Was he alluding to her solitary pilgrimage to England? Her clothes? She searched his face for a clue and saw, beneath the anger, a mix of deeper feelings: resentment, disappointment, frustration. A natural reaction, she decided. Jeffrey could accept the unknown relative who stood between him and his inheritance, but now "Cousin Robert" was here—flaunting his position, oozing pleasantries, insulting Jeffrey's father—his simmering hostility had boiled to the surface. And perhaps it was also natural that he should direct that hostility to her. She ached to comfort him, to tell him the truth, but the memory of Mr. Wilcox's menacing eyes hung between them.

"I am sorry," she murmured instead.

"Sorry?" Jeffrey's own eyes sparked with interest.

"Yes. I wish I could explain . . ." Her voice trailed lamely off.

"Never mind." His face had gone blank—all the emotion drained away—and he sounded very tired. "No explanation is required. To the contrary, your motives have become abundantly clear, and I fear my embarrassment is equally clear to you. It's painful for a man to own that a woman has successfully deceived him."

Deceived? Kate entertained a brief, wild hope that Jeffrey had penetrated her masquerade. Her dilemma would be resolved, and Mr. Wilcox could not hold her responsible . . . But he could. Her stomach knotted with panic, and she licked her lips. Mr. Wilcox would assume she had betrayed him and wreak swift and terrible revenge.

"I . . . I don't understand," she croaked aloud.

"I believed your high-flown talk of love. Indeed,

as you may recollect, I was quite worried about you." Jeffrey laughed—a low, harsh sound devoid of merriment. "I feared you would persuade yourself that you were in love with Gilbert and come to realize too late that you were not. Was that your objective, Kate? I am still somewhat puzzled in that regard. Were you attempting to enlist my sympathy for the Naive Young Bride Forced to Wed a Stranger?"

He might have been reciting the title of a bad play, and Kate shook her head. "No! I—"

"Never mind," he repeated. "Your previous conduct no longer signifies. As I indicated earlier, your motives have grown perfectly clear. Your sole concern is for wealth and position, and you have put yourself to a great deal of trouble to secure them. It almost seems a pity—"

There was a rustle at the rear entry of the dining room, and when Kate spun her head, she saw Adams bustling over the threshold.

"I am sorry, sir." The butler ground to an apologetic halt and signaled the footmen behind him to stop as well. "I fancied you were finished."

"We are finished." Jeffrey leapt to his feet and flung his napkin on the tablecloth, directly into the spreading pool of blancmange. "I have nothing more to say to *Cousin Kate*."

He stared at her for an endless moment, his eyes colder and harder than Mr. Wilcox's. Then he whirled around and stalked into the foyer, and though the servants proceeded into the room and began to clear the table, Kate had never before felt so utterly alone.

10

"The charge," the judge said sternly, "is that you posed for some weeks as Kitty Sinclair, the daughter of the late Lord Latimer. His lordship's relatives are seeking fifteen thousand pounds in recompense."

He looked down, leafing through the papers on the bench, and his wig slipped over his right eye. Despite the gravity of the situation, Kate could not repress a giggle.

"It is not amusing, Miss Morrow." The judge looked coldly up and adjusted his wig. "As you can see for yourself, the injured parties are most distressed."

Kate glanced over her shoulder, but they did not appear in the least distressed to her. For some reason, the proceedings were being held at Almack's, and everyone was dancing: Jeffrey with Miss Dalton, Lady Latimer with Mr. Wilcox, and Gilbert with his Aunt Agnes.

"Furthermore," the judge went on, "a number of merchants in Leicester Square have filed claims as well."

He picked up a scroll and began to unroll it, but it soon exceeded the length of his arms. The bottom of the scroll fell to the floor and continued to unroll, yard after yard, until it became entangled in the feet of the dancers.

"How do you intend to pay the damages?" the judge demanded.

"I do not intend to pay them." Kate giggled

again. "I have no money, sir. Perhaps you will have to send me to Bedlam."

"I wish I could, Miss Morrow," the judge said heavily. "Unfortunately, however, the penalty for fraud is death."

"Death!" Kate gasped.

"Did you not understand that when you embarked on your charade?" The judge sorrowfully shook his head. "I am required by law to order your execution, but I shall allow you to select the method. You may choose starvation in the streets of London or beheading at the Tower. I personally recommend the latter course, for you will be in excellent company. Anne Boleyn, King Charles the First . . ."

Kate's eyes flew open, and she bolted upright, expecting to find herself in a cold, damp cell. But she was in her comfortable bed in Charles Street, and she heaved a tremulous sigh of relief. The last beheading in England had taken place nearly seventy years since, and no one had been imprisoned in the Tower for decades.

Kate wriggled to the headboard and propped a pillow behind her back. Mrs. Todhunter's cook had also claimed to have prophetic dreams, and Kate did not deny that such a thing was possible. However, she herself possessed no psychic powers, and her dreams—when they had any meaning at all—tended to clarify the present. Their very absurdity, she had learned, often revealed a truth she had failed to perceive during her waking hours.

And this dream was a splendid example. Mr. Wilcox had threatened her with prison or worse if she attempted to expose him, and Kate had been so startled and confused that she believed him. She now recognized how hollow his threats were:

as ridiculous as the prospect of her execution on
Tower Green. There was no question that—all else
being equal—his story would be the more
credible. But Mr. Wilcox had cleverly intimidated
her into forgetting that all else was *not* equal.
Quite the reverse, in fact; it was to Jeffrey's
advantage to accept her version of events.

Indeed, Kate thought with growing optimism, if
a perfect stranger knocked at the door and
whispered that "Cousin Robert" was an impostor,
Jeffrey would be compelled to investigate. And she
was far from being a stranger. Jeffrey had clearly
implied that were it not for his honor, he would
undertake to court her, and his outburst last
evening was further evidence of his affection. He
would not care a deuce for her motives if he did
not also care for her. She need only be honest with
him, and he would protect her from Mr. Wilcox.

So perhaps Mr. Wilcox's arrival was really a
blessing in disguise. Kate crossed her arms behind
her head and—as she had in her dream—emitted a
little giggle. Jeffrey would be shocked to learn of
her masquerade, but surely her confession would
serve to prove that she had never intended any
harm. Between them, they would give Mr. Wilcox
a proper setdown, and thirty years hence, they
would merrily relate the tale to their grand-
children—

The mantel clock chimed twice, and Kate bolted
up again. It was half past eight, she saw with
dismay. Lady Latimer would be waiting to escort
her to Mrs. Copeland's, and she must speak with
Jeffrey before she left. She leapt out of bed,
donned the least offensive of her walking dresses,
and hurried to the dining room.

"There you are!" Miss Dalton said. "I was
beginning to fear you'd been stricken ill as well."

"As well?" Kate echoed. Miss Dalton was alone, she observed, gazing round the room. "Is everyone else sick?"

"Your father is still alseep. It's Lady Latimer who is sick."

"And Jeffrey?" Kate asked. "Where is Jeffrey?"

"He set out for Brooks's a few minutes since."

Kate clenched her hands with frustration; their conversation would have to be postponed. But after they spoke, he would be spared the daily pilgrimage to his club. Yes, once Jeffrey knew the truth, everything would change.

"Lady Latimer sent word with Sally that her cold is worse," Miss Dalton continued. "As she mentioned last night, she doesn't wish to be ill for her ball, and she judges it best to conserve her strength. She consequently suggested that we proceed to Mrs. Copeland's alone."

"*We*?" Kate repeated. "You are going with me?" She bit her lip. She had hoped to avoid Miss Dalton as much as possible, but that was no excuse for rudeness.

"Yes." Miss Dalton nodded; fortunately, she did not appear to have registered Kate's tone. "Now I've seen the current London styles, I fancy I could use a few new gowns myself. Country fashions tend to be nearly as outmoded as those in the colonies."

Her black eyes darted from the collarless bodice of Kate's dress to the plain ruffle around the skirt, and Kate clenched her hands again.

"Are you ready then?" Miss Dalton pushed her plate away and stood up. "Jeffrey ordered out the carriage before he left."

Evidently she failed to recollect that Kate had not had a single bite of breakfast. But that was all right, Kate conceded; she was far too nervous to

be hungry. She sped into the vestibule and
snatched her new French bonnet off the pier table.
At least it was not "outmoded," she thought as she
tied the satin ribbons. She plucked up her gloves
and trailed Miss Dalton out the door and across
the footpath to the landau.

It was not far from Charles Street to Leicester
Square; Kate and Lady Latimer had accomplished
the drive in under fifteen minutes. But the traffic
in Piccadilly was unusually heavy this morning,
and the carriage soon slowed to a veritable crawl.
At this rate, Kate calculated, the journey would
require half an hour or more, and the silence was
already beginning to grow oppressive. She cleared
her throat.

"Do you visit London often, Miss Dalton?"

"I wish you would call me Barbara." Miss
Dalton had been watching the traffic on her side of
the carriage, and she now transferred her
attention to Kate. "We are likely to see a great
deal of each other in the years to come."

Kate strongly doubted this. Miss Dalton was
already sensitive about her father's lack of title,
and she would feel it very hard indeed when
Jeffrey jilted her. So hard that she would probably
decline to associate with her former *parti*, much
less befriend his wife. But there was no point in
welcoming trouble before it arrived.

"Barbara," she agreed.

The landau advanced a yard or two, and
Barbara sighed. "My conscience has been teasing
me since last evening," she said, "and I daresay it
will continue to do so until I apologize."

"Apologize?" Kate knit a frown of puzzlement.
She had disliked Miss Dalton from the start, but
the fault for that was hers. Insofar as she could
recall, Barbara had said nothing, done nothing,
overtly offensive.

"Yes. From the time we met, I doubted you were Kate Sinclair."

"Not . . . not Kate Sinclair?" Kate stammered. She had been taken utterly by surprise. "How . . . however did you conceive such a notion?"

"Your height, to begin with. As you might imagine, I have a keen interest in height." Barbara sketched a wry smile. "Lord Halstead's description had led me to suppose you were nearly as tall as I. And then there was the matter of the *Exeter*. Grandpapa may have exaggerated their peril, but even Papa is persuaded that the voyage was excessively harrowing. I could scarcely believe you had never heard the story."

"I . . . I see." Kate could not seem to stop stuttering. "What did you fancy had become of the real Kate?" It was a dangerous question, but her curiosity overcame her discretion.

"She might have died. I understand that the climate of Bermuda is most unhealthy. Or she might have fallen in love with someone else and refused to marry Gilbert."

Kate kept her face carefully blank.

"At any rate," Barbara continued, "I went so far as to search your bedchamber."

"You?" Kate gasped. "It was you?"

"You noticed then." Barbara ruefully shook her head. "I tried to put everything back in order, but I was in a fearful hurry. I hoped that if you did notice, you'd assume Sally had tidied up your clothes."

Kate elected not to reveal what she had really assumed.

"I found nothing, of course," Barbara said. "And now your father has arrived, there is no longer any doubt of your identity. That is what concerned me, you see. You wouldn't dare to pose as Kate Sinclair unless something had happened to Lord Latimer. Unless he was dead or so near death that he couldn't communicate with his family. In which case, your impersonation would delay Jeffrey's inheritance."

Good God! Kate struggled to maintain her composure. "Did you discuss your suspicions with him?" she asked as casually as she could. "With Jeffrey, that is?"

"No. As I said, I found no proof. To the contrary, Lord Latimer's arrival has proved me altogether wrong. I can only pray you will forgive me."

Kate choked down another wild giggle. Far from being wrong, Barbara had deduced the situation so accurately that it seemed unfair to deceive her a moment more. But perhaps Jeffrey would want to keep Kate's information confidential until he had obtained irrefutable evidence of Mr. Wilcox's imposture.

"I forgive you," she murmured aloud.

"And you will put it all behind you? I do want us to be friends, Kate. As everyone is so fond of pointing out, we have a great deal in common. More than you know. When I met your father, my first impression was that he is very much like mine."

"Umm," Kate grunted.

Her guilt was increasing with every passing second, and she glanced out the carriage window. They had made considerable progress, she saw— they were drawn up just opposite the Haymarket —but it was still several minutes to Leicester Square. Much too far to finish the drive in silence.

"They look alike, you mean?" She shifted her eyes back to Barbara.

"Oh, no, they look nothing alike. Papa is tall, but he's quite lean and very dark. I was referring to their mannerisms. It's apparent from his bearing that Lord Latimer is also a successful man of business. And he seems as eager as my father to wed his daughter to a peer."

"Umm," Kate growled again. "I believe the traffic is starting to thin at last—"

"Your father emerged much the better on that head, of course: he will wed you to an earl, and he became a viscount himself. My papa will have to wait for his patience to be rewarded."

Wait for your papa to die, Kate translated. It was an exceedingly tactless remark, and despite the circumstances, she felt a stab of vexation.

"But you mustn't think badly of Papa." Barbara might have been reading Kate's thoughts. "He would much prefer me to marry someone who already has a title, but I insisted only Jeffrey would do. So Papa has agreed to announce our engagement at Lady Latimer's ball."

Her words had the force of a physical blow—a fist slamming unexpectedly into Kate's stomach. "Engagement?" she choked. "At . . . the . . . ball?" She barely had the breath to speak.

"I hope you don't mind. I hate to intrude on your and Gilbert's grand moment, but Jeffrey regards Lady Latimer almost as a mother. She'd be terribly wounded if we announced our betrothal anywhere else."

"No," Kate croaked.

Or did she? There was a peculiar buzzing in her ears, making it difficult for her to hear Barbara, hear herself—difficult even to think. The landau stopped, and when she gazed out the window, she realized that her vision was clouded as well. Had they reached Mrs. Copeland's shop? Evidently so, for the blurred form of Drake, the coachman, soon opened the door and handed her out. The footpath seemed to roll beneath her feet, tilting and buckling till she was hard put to maintain her balance. She had never experienced an earthquake, but she fancied it must create a similar sensation.

"Come along." Barbara seized Kate's wrist and tugged her on across the footpath. "And don't say anything to Mrs. Copeland," she whispered over her shoulder. "She's a dreadful gossip, and I wish to keep our engagement a secret until the assembly."

"Miss Sinclair?" The dowdy little mantua-maker was dressing one of the mannequins in the window, but she peered up at the sound of the bell. "And Miss Dalton!" She bounded forward to greet them. "It is an honor to serve you again."

Honor. Kate's mind abruptly cleared, and she chided herself for her stupidity. She had based all her plans on Jeffrey's honor, and she hadn't understood what he meant. He had not been alluding to her engagement; he had been warning her of his own obligation to marry Barbara.

"Maria will show you the stylebook, Miss Dalton." Mrs. Copeland beckoned to her assistant, who was desultorily dusting one of the gilt chairs. "Meanwhile, I shall fit Miss Sinclair's clothes. Come with me, Miss Sinclair."

She strode toward the rear of the shop, and Kate stumbled after her. What was she to do now? she wondered, her brain beginning to spin again. Mrs. Copeland deftly unhooked her dress, pulled it over her head, and assisted her into a walking costume. If she revealed Mr. Wilcox's imposture, Jeffrey would be grateful . . .

"I believe the spencer is a trifle tight through the bosom," Mrs. Copeland said.

"Yes," Kate muttered absently, glancing into the cheval glass.

Grateful enough that he would still protect her from Mr. Wilcox. But . . .

"Will you look at this!" Mrs. Copeland snapped.

Kate started and returned her attention to the mirror. The walking dress had miraculously vanished, and she was wearing the ball gown with the blue satin corsage.

"The sleeves are much too loose." Mrs. Copeland's eyes blazed with irritation. "I shall be extremely annoyed if Maria measured your arms incorrectly."

But if she exposed Mr. Wilcox, she must expose herself as well. And then . . .

"Fortunately, she did not." Mrs. Copeland heaved a sigh of relief. "You see, Miss Sinclair? This is how the sleeves *should* fit." The blue gown had been supplanted by the gold one. "I daresay my seamstresses didn't do the slashes properly."

And then where would she be? Once Mr. Wilcox had slunk back to Bermuda, Jeffrey's protection would cease. Sooner or later . . .

"I am sorry, Miss Sinclair."

"Sorry?" The apple-green morning dress appeared to fit quite perfectly.

"You didn't feel it then. I feared I had jabbed your ankle with a pin. The dress is a bit long, don't you agree?"

Sooner or later, she would starve in the streets after all. She had lost Jeffrey, and Gilbert wouldn't wed her without a dowry . . .

"Well, that is it," Mrs. Copeland said briskly. She helped Kate out of the last ball gown and returned it to the rack. "As I promised Lady Latimer, I shall deliver everything on Friday. Now, if you will pardon me, I shall record Miss Dalton's order while you dress."

Miss Dalton's order, Kate thought bitterly. Part of a real trousseau . . .

The rest of the morning passed in a blur: a disjointed series of incidents with great gaps

between them. Kate clearly remembered an interminable debate about gloves; would the white or
the straw-colored better complement the peach
walking dress Barbara had ordered? Eventually—
"to be safe"—she purchased both. But what else
had she bought? Kate wondered when she
chanced to notice Drake again. Somehow, as if by
magic, three or four additional parcels had
materialized in his arms.

"Are you going to inquire about the toque?"
Barbara asked.

"Toque?" Kate echoed dumbly. "What toque?"

"The Kent toque you admired. The one Lady
Latimer mentioned. This is the milliner she
normally patronizes."

So it was, Kate saw; they had made their way
nearly round the square. She glanced up and spied
the toque on a shelf behind the counter. "No," she
mumbled. "I don't believe I care for it after all."

"Then if you'll be patient a few minutes more, I
should like to try on the leghorn hat."

A few minutes, a few hours—Kate had no notion
how much time had elapsed when they emerged
from the shop. Apparently Barbara had purchased
the hat, for she placed still another box in Drake's
arms. But it could as easily have been some other
bonnet; Kate had no memory of that either.

Nor of the homeward drive. She was vaguely
aware that they were delayed by traffic between
Bond Street and Berkeley, but she didn't realize
they had reached Lady Latimer's house until she
found herself on the footpath.

"Are you all right, miss?" Drake frowned down
at her.

"Yes! Yes, I am waiting for Miss Dalton."

"Miss Dalton has already gone in." His frown
deepened. "We had quite a long discussion about

her packages. She insisted on taking them
herself." He indicated the empty seats inside the
carriage.

"I fancy I dozed off," Kate said weakly.
"Shopping is quite exhausting, Drake. No one
should know that better than yourself."

She hurried across the footpath and up the steps
and slipped through the open door. With any luck,
she could avoid the rest of the household until she
sorted out her jumbled thoughts—

"Here she is!" Mr. Wilcox was standing in the
library doorway, Gilbert beside him. "And *she* has
no parcels, Gilbert. Miss Dalton was so burdened
she could scarcely stagger up the staircase.
Perhaps my lecture had some effect."

Barbara was right, Kate reflected distantly: he
was a brilliant man of business. With one double
entendre, undetectable to Gilbert, he had cleverly
reminded her of her precarious situation. The one
bright spot in this long, awful day was that he
couldn't possibly know how effective the
reminder was. And she would not give him that
satisfaction—not now and not ever.

"My clothes will be delivered Friday," she
rejoined coolly.

"And the bills not long thereafter, I'll warrant."
Mr. Wilcox laughed. "Keep in mind, Gilbert, that I
shall pay them when they come. Now, if you will
excuse me, I have not entirely recovered from my
journey. I daresay I should rest before this
evening's festivities." He granted them a cordial
smile and retreated up the stairs.

"It is the least he can do," Gilbert muttered.

"I beg your pardon?" Kate shook her head; she
must attempt to concentrate.

"The least he can do is pay for your trousseau."
The earl was glaring in Mr. Wilcox's wake. "I
called on your father to discuss your dowry, and

he is driving a very hard bargain. He claims that the Bermudian property he pledged has substantially increased in value . . ."

Gilbert stopped and shook his own head. "Forgive me. It is most improper of me to involve you in our negotiations. I should simply like to know . . ." His voice trailed off again.

"Know what?" Kate pressed.

"If I am wasting my time and Lord Latimer's as well. I did not advise him that we regard our engagement as tentative. If you wish to cry off, I should like to know at once, before I debate your father for every last groat."

There it was—the question that had tormented Kate from the moment she left Mrs. Copeland's shop. She did not love Gilbert, but the man she did love was committed to someone else. If, in fact, she loved him. Jeffrey would undoubtedly contend that her feelings were nothing more than an infatuation, and perhaps he was correct. Perhaps, six months hence, she would look back and marvel that she could have conceived such a foolish schoolgirl *tendre*.

But that didn't signify. Six months hence, Jeffrey would be wed to Barbara. Kate could no longer weigh him against Gilbert; she must compare Gilbert to an unknown alternative. Gilbert was handsome and pleasant, and he had a splendid title. One title now, and excellent prospects of succeeding to another. He was not rich, but when the income from her dowry was added to that of his estates, they could live quite comfortably. As Mr. Wilcox had pointed out, she was unlikely to make a better match. Indeed, if she revealed her masquerade, she was unlikely to make any match at all.

"There is obviously a question in your mind," Gilbert said. "The same as that in mine, I fancy.

Let us not hide our teeth, Kate. I shan't pretend to be mad for you, and you needn't affect undying passion either. We agreed to wed if we found ourselves compatible, and I daresay we shall get on well enough."

He was echoing Jeffrey: compatability—*getting on*—was the best one could expect.

"I daresay we shall," Kate murmured aloud. "And I should be . . . be honored to have our engagement announced at Cousin Jane's ball."

That sounded like Jeffrey as well. Would she be thinking of Jeffrey the rest of her life?

"If your father and I can come to terms by then," Gilbert said grimly. "But that is not your concern." He clapped his beaver hat on his head. "I shall see you tonight."

He bowed, strode across the vestibule, let himself out; and Kate fled up the staircase. She was thoroughly winded by the time she reached the second story, and as she sagged against the newel post, the door on the opposite side of the landing creaked open.

"There you are," Mr. Wilcox hissed. "I was wondering what had delayed you. I trust nothing is amiss?"

"Amiss?" Kate panted. Everything was amiss. "I have consented to marry Gilbert if that is what you mean."

"An excellent decision." Mr. Wilcox essayed his paternal smile. "But scarcely surprising. You're an extremely clever girl, and I was confident you would see on which side your bread was buttered. You look a trifle tired, dear. You should also try to rest before the evening."

He closed the door, and Kate ground her teeth with fury. If only there were some way to set him down, she thought, trudging on along the corridor.

Some means of eating her cake and having it too . . .

But there was. Her fingers froze to the knob of her bedchamber door. A way so simple she was astonished Mr. Wilcox hadn't perceived it himself. She would wed Gilbert, and once he had safely secured her dowry, she would reveal the truth. At that juncture, she would be a countess—possibly a marchioness—and no one would care who she had been prior to her marriage. Jeffrey would come into his inheritance, and Barbara would share in his good fortune. Only Mr. Wilcox would suffer, and that was as it should be.

Yes, it was a splendid solution. Kate opened the door and stepped into her room. A *perfect* solution, and she could not conceive why her cheeks were wet with tears.

11

"Mrs. Copeland should be hanged!" Lady Latimer snapped. "Did you notice, dear, that Barbara's gown is almost *exactly* like yours?"

Kate had forgotten what she was wearing, and she glanced down. The sapphire satin, she saw, and when she looked back to the spot where Barbara and Jeffrey were waltzing, she observed that Barbara's dress was, indeed, similar. The bodice was green rather than blue, but the sleeves were identically slashed, and the skirts of both gowns were white lace over satin. However, the drapery of roses round Barbara's skirt was wider, and Mrs. Copeland had added an extra rouleau above it and below. These differences, while minor, served to make Barbara appear even taller and more graceful than she was. She smiled up at Jeffrey, and Kate clenched her hands.

"They are a handsome couple, are they not?" Lady Latimer sighed.

"Yes," Kate muttered.

"You and Gilbert are a handsome couple too, of course," her ladyship added hastily. She peered at the far corner of the ballroom, where the earl and Mr. Wilcox were deep in conversation. "Though I do wish he would grant you a bit more attention. One would think he and Cousin Robert could discuss your . . . ah . . ." She stopped and cleared her throat. "Could discuss their business during the day."

One would think so did one not know Mr. Wilcox, Kate reflected grimly. Everyone in the household had recognized by now that their "business" was that of her dowry, and everyone was undoubtedly wondering what could be taking so long. Mr. Wilcox and Gilbert had conferred every afternoon—not excluding Sunday, when they had repaired to the library for several hours following church and midday dinner—but their interminable negotiations spilled into the evenings as well. Kate had collected from Mr. Wilcox's brief progress reports and the earl's increasingly harried expression that their conversations much resembled water dripping on a stone. No single drop did discernible damage, but patiently, relentlessly, Mr. Wilcox was eroding the rock of Gilbert's resistance.

"I hope they will finish by Saturday," Lady Latimer said nervously.

Saturday! Kate's heart crashed against her ribs.

Where had the time gone? It was like water on stone again: each hour had seemed to last forever, but nearly a week had been chipped away. It was already Monday, and in five short days, her engagement would be announced.

"I am sure they will," she murmured aloud. Mr. Wilcox would not put his whole plan at risk for fifty pounds here or a hundred there.

"Do not tease yourself about it, dear." Lady Latimer patted Kate's shoulder. "Gilbert's concern for the financial settlement in no way indicates a lack of affection. To the contrary, he is eager to ensure your mutual future. Horace's demands were so extreme that at one point, my father terminated their negotiations altogether. But they ultimately came to terms, and Horace and I lived quite happily for two-and-thirty years . . ."

Kate closed her ears to her ladyship's chatter and gazed around Lord Fordham's ballroom. No, she remembered, this was Lady Pemberton's ballroom; they had attended Lord Fordham's rout on Friday. No, they had gone to the theater Friday; Lord Fordham's assembly must have been Saturday. How ironic. She narrowly repressed a mocking laugh. Her wildest dreams had come to pass—she was mingling with the very pink of the *ton*, and she was soon to wed an earl—but her triumph tasted like ashes on her tongue. Earlier in the day, she had chanced to leaf through Lady Latimer's latest copy of *Ackermann's Repository*, and it had occurred to her that she much resembled one of the models. Clad in her new finery, she had been paraded about night after night, an empty smile on her mouth—

The music stopped, and Jeffrey bowed to Barbara and took her elbow to escort her off the floor. Kate carefully arranged her face in the blank, pleasant expression she had mastered so well.

"Your dress is lovely, dear," Lady Latimer cooed, now patting Barbara's shoulder. "I'm sure no one else will notice that it's quite similar to Kate's—"

"Miss Dalton!" Lady Kemble trotted up behind Lady Latimer. "I am enormously comforted to see you. I trust your presence in town indicates that your dear mother is improved?"

"Yes." Barbara stepped forward to greet Lady Kemble. "Mama is much better, thank you . . ."

The three women began to chat, leaving Kate and Jeffrey effectively alone. She stared straight ahead, her glassy smile in place.

"Your gown is lovely as well," Jeffrey said politely.

Did he sound a trifle warmer than he had these six days past? Kate looked eagerly up at him and immediately regretted it. His tone had meant nothing, she saw; his demeanor was the cold, forbidding one he had displayed since the night of Mr. Wilcox's arrival. Indeed, she fancied Jeffrey's attitude was the most distressing aspect of her whole abysmal situation.

Kate dropped her eyes and clenched her hands again. She had assumed that—having made the decision to wed Barbara—Jeffrey would put his bitterness aside. As Barbara had pointed out, the two couples were likely to spend a great deal of time together in the coming years, and all of them stood to benefit if the relationship was a harmonious one. But Jeffrey's conduct had been far from harmonious. He had taken great pains to avoid Kate, and when circumstance thrust them together, his frosty manner suggested that she had somehow betrayed him. *She* had betrayed *him*? He had known from the start that she was engaged

to Gilbert. He was the one who had suddenly
elected to have his own betrothal announced . . .

But there was no point in assessing blame.
Particularly not now; the silence was growing
strained. Kate forced her eyes back up.

"Thank you," she mumbled.

"Gilbert and Cousin Robert are still at it, I see."
Jeffrey glanced across the ballroom, and Kate
tried to read his expression, but there was nothing
to read. He looked—and sounded—as though he
had peered idly out a window and noticed a
change in the weather. Perhaps he was beginning
to overcome his bitterness after all.

"Y-yes." She could not seem to raise her voice
above a mutter.

"You mean to go through with it then." He
looked abruptly back at her. "You mean to marry
Gilbert."

There it was again: the implication that she had
wronged him. His eyes were cold and hard and yet
—behind their icy glitter—faintly wounded. It is
not my fault! she wanted to shriek. You left me no
alternative . . . But it was too late, much too late,
for that.

"You were aware of my obligation to Gilbert,"
she rejoined as levelly as she could. "You understood the situation before . . ." She had started to
say before I did, and she bit her lip. "Before we
met," she concluded instead.

"If only I had." Jeffrey emitted a short,
humorless laugh and gazed once more across the
ballroom.

"Please, Jeffrey," Kate whispered. "I know you
are excessively distressed. But one day—one day
soon . . ." She stopped and chose her words with
care. "Everything will be clear. And when it is, I
hope we can be friends."

"I think not, Kate." His voice was flat, and his

eyes—when they returned to her—were empty. "At one time, I entertained foolish hopes of my own. I fancied that . . ." He stopped as well and shook his head. "No, we can never be friends."

It was not a rude remark; she could have countered rudeness with an equally nasty retort. But Jeffrey seemed to be stating an unfortunate, inescapable fact, and she had no immediate answer for that. She was still groping for the proper response when Barbara and Lady Latimer bustled up beside them.

"What a tiresome woman!" Barbara hissed.

Kate peered past her and observed Lady Kemble galloping toward another knot of guests.

"That she is," Lady Latimer agreed. "But Lord Kemble is extremely prominent in the House, and one can't afford to offend her. You did very well, dear." She beamed approvingly at Barbara.

"Then I daresay I am entitled to reward myself with a glass of champagne. Will you join me, Jeffrey?"

She linked her arm through his and tugged him away, and Kate stared enviously after them. It was a casual gesture, but—perhaps for that very reason—infinitely possessive.

"Are you ill, dear?" Lady Latimer said sharply.

"No!" Kate started and donned her vacant smile. "I'm a bit distracted this evening."

"You are distracted because you are ill." Lady Latimer stripped off her right glove and laid the back of her hand on Kate's brow. "Just as I suspected. You are feverish, and you must go home at once."

"No," Kate repeated. "I feel quite well."

"You *think* you feel well, but it is obvious to me that you are catching my cold. And you must not be sick Saturday night. Had I ignored my symptoms, I should probably still be abed.

Fortunately, you are young, and with a good night's sleep, you will probably be recovered by tomorrow. I shall desire Drake to take you home immediately."

Her ladyship spun around and promptly collided with Mr. Wilcox. He was looking very pleased with himself, Kate noted, and Gilbert was looking more harried than ever.

"Humph," Lady Latimer sniffed. "If you will pardon me for saying so, Cousin Robert, you really should have more care for Kate's health. The poor child is coming down with a cold, and I was just at the point of sending her home. I am sure you will wish to accompany her. Gilbert can take the rest of us up in his carriage."

Mr. Wilcox sketched a little frown of vexation, but even he could not withstand Lady Latimer when her mind was made up. He offered Kate his arm and began to escort her toward the ballroom entry.

"Give her a brandy," her ladyship called after them, "and then insist she go directly to bed."

Mr. Wilcox nodded and ushered Kate on out of the ballroom and down the stairs to the ground story. The street was a veritable sea of carriages, but by a great stroke of luck, Lady Latimer's landau was situated only a few yards from the door. Drake and several of his fellow coachmen were conducting a party of their own, Kate observed: flasks were hastily shoved into pockets as she and Mr. Wilcox approached, and Drake's hands were a trifle unsteady when he assisted her up the step. But he mounted the box quite nimbly and turned the carriage round without apparent difficulty.

"A cold?" Mr. Wilcox snapped. "You do not seem ill to me. You are scarcely behaving like a happy bride, my dear."

"I am not a happy bride," Kate snapped back. "And it was Lady Latimer who conceived the notion that I'm ill—"

"Never mind." He waved her to silence. "Happy or no, you *will* be a bride. Young Halstead and I have finally reached agreement."

"I was confident you would," Kate said acidly.

"And a very favorable agreement at that. I shall have to confirm my calculations on paper, but I believe I reduced the settlement to twelve thousand pounds."

Which meant there would be less for her and Gilbert to live on, Kate thought. But she was an excellent financial manager; she had snatched Papa from the brink of bankruptcy half a dozen times. She could readily reduce expenses by a few hundred pounds a year. Mr. Wilcox launched into a cheerful, tuneless whistle, and Kate once more closed her ears and gazed out the carriage window.

There was no traffic at this time of night, and the drive from Manchester Square to Charles Street required under ten minutes. Neither she nor Mr. Wilcox had a key to the house, Kate belatedly recalled, and no one answered her ring. She started to ring again, then further recollected that Lady Latimer had given Adams permission to retire early. The butler truly was catching her ladyship's cold; he had been coughing and sneezing all day. Kate twisted the knob and discovered, to her relief, that the door was unlocked.

"Brandy, my dear?" Mr. Wilcox said, following her into the vestibule. "I did promise Cousin Jane to give you a brandy."

"No, thank you. I am not sick—"

"But we must toast our victory," he interposed. "Come along."

His victory, Kate corrected bitterly. But there was no reason to create unnecessary dissension. To the contrary; her revenge would all be the sweeter if it took him entirely unawares. She trailed him obediently through the library doorway, and he strode to the liquor cabinet, poured two glasses, stepped back across the room, and handed one of the glasses to her.

"To us." He raised his glass, then drained half the contents in one great gulp.

Kate sipped from her own glass, but the taste was quite as awful as she remembered. Like Lady Latimer, Papa had occasionally prescribed brandy for medicinal purposes, but Kate had always fancied it more likely to kill than cure. How could it be healthful? In addition to tasting horrid, it seared one's throat, burned one's stomach . . . Fortunately, she had taken only a tiny mouthful, and she choked it down and placed her glass on the sofa table.

"During the course of our negotiations, Gilbert chanced to remark that the town house is not a part of the Latimer entailment." Mr. Wilcox was peering round the library. "So I daresay I shall have to purchase a city home for myself."

"I daresay you will." It would enhance the setdown, Kate reflected gleefully. Perhaps she could persuade him to hold a grand house-warming and publicly expose him before all the assembled *ton*.

"Indeed, I have been thinking." He swallowed another generous portion of brandy. "Did Robert mention that I've never married?"

"No, he did not."

"I was so preoccupied with business that I lacked the time for courting. But now I'm a man of leisure, I rather fancy the notion of a wife. In view of my title, I expect I could wed a woman of considerable fortune. And if I selected a younger woman, I might yet become a father."

Kate entertained a vision of Mr. Wilcox skulking back to Bermuda with an enraged young wife and squalling infant in tow. The prospect was so delicious that she could scarcely keep her countenance.

"Maybe so," she said, quelling a giggle. "We must discuss it further—"

The doorbell pealed, and she and Mr. Wilcox simultaneously started. It was an excessively odd hour to be calling, and Kate surmised that someone had mistaken Lady Latimer's house for another. Perhaps one of the neighbors had invited guests— The bell rang again, and she recollected that Adams was asleep. Asleep and ill; it wouldn't do for him to be disturbed

"I shall see who it is," she said.

She hurried across the vestibule, threw the door open, and sagged against it. She might be looking at a portrait of herself, she thought through a haze of shock. An ill-executed portrait: the young woman on the doorstep was much taller than she, and her eyes were a vivid emerald green. But her face, though a trifle rounder, was astonishingly similar to Kate's, and her hair was precisely the same shade of blond.

"Who is it?" Mr. Wilcox called.

Kate parted her lips, but no sound came; she had once more been stricken dumb.

"Did you answer the door or not?" he demanded querulously.

She heard the tap of his footfalls in the library, in the foyer behind her, and then the sharp intake of his breath.

"Kitty?" he gasped. "What the devil are you doing here?"

12

The three of them stood in silence for ten full seconds; Kate could hear the ticking of the clock in the rear hall. Characteristically, Mr. Wilcox was the first to recover.

"But what am I thinking of?" He bounded forward and seized Kitty's elbow. "You must be exhausted, my dear. Come in and have a glass of brandy."

"Uncle Samuel?" She shook her head as if to clear it. "Mr. Glover told me you'd gone to England, but I didn't expect to find you here."

"I shall explain everything in due time," he said soothingly. "Come along now."

He tugged her over the threshold, and when Kate peered past them, she observed a hackney coach in the street. The driver soon panted up the front steps, bearing a trunk on one shoulder and carrying a valise in his opposite hand.

"The lady's luggage," he wheezed, reaching the door.

"Put it here."

Mr. Wilcox waved vaguely round the foyer, and the driver stepped inside and deposited both cases on the marble floor.

"The lady's fare is half a pound, sir."

"That is nonsense, and you know it," Mr. Wilcox snapped. He extracted a purse from the pocket of his evening coat and withdrew a coin. "You'll accept five shillings and be happy with that."

The driver did, in fact, accept the coin, but he

was far from happy: he stalked back through the door and crashed it resoundingly to in his wake.

"Come along now," Mr. Wilcox repeated. "I'm sure you've had an extremely tiring journey. I collect you took the stage from Plymouth?"

He led Kitty toward the library doorway, and— her curiosity fairly bubbling over—Kate trailed after them.

"Yes." Kitty wearily bobbed her head. "I thought it would be about the same distance as from St. George's to Hamilton, but I've been on the road for hours and hours."

"Of course you have," Mr. Wilcox clucked. He seated her solicitously on the couch, snatched Kate's glass off the sofa table, and thrust it into Kitty's hand. "Have a sip of this, dear. Brandy is a wonderful restorative."

Kitty obediently drank from the glass and succumbed to a fit of frenzied coughing. But evidently she did not judge the alleged restorative as distasteful as Kate did, for she took another sip at once.

"I trust you will forgive me if I sounded rude." Mr. Wilcox sank into the shield-back chair across from the couch. "Naturally, I was quite surprised to see you. I had supposed you were settled in Virginia by now."

"Virginia!" Kitty's cheeks flooded with color. "I should have listened to Papa. He warned me that Thomas would be a most unsatisfactory husband, but I refused to heed him. Until Thomas and I reached Richmond."

She swallowed another portion of brandy and slammed the glass back on the table. "I assumed Thomas would give up his seafaring once we were wed, but he had no such intention. And that wasn't the worst of it. He planned for me to live with his mother while he sailed off for months at a time. She was a dragon, I can tell you."

"How unfortunate," Mr. Wilcox murmured.

"That it was." Kitty's green eyes blazed with indignation. "A week of her company was more than I could bear, and I returned to Bermuda on the next ship. I went directly from the dock to your office, thinking to apologize to Papa, and Mr. Glover informed me that he had . . . had . . ."

She affected a dramatic sniffle, but Kate noticed that her eyes were quite undimmed by tears.

"My poor child." Mr. Wilcox sorrowfully shook his head. "What happened after that?"

"As I stated earlier, Mr. Glover also advised me that you had gone to England. You anticipated an extended absence, he said, and had appointed him to operate the business in your stead. I counted that a wise decision. Papa always maintained that Mr. Glover was the best of your assistants—"

"Yes, yes." A note of impatience had crept beneath Mr. Wilcox's soothing tone. "I was asking why *you* decided to come to England."

"I fancied I could best honor Papa's memory by wedding Lord Halstead's son after all." Kitty essayed another sniffle and retrieved her brandy glass.

It was the stuff of high comedy, Kate thought, repressing an hysterical giggle. Vastly more amusing than the play they had attended Friday evening. She glanced from Kitty to Mr. Wilcox, eagerly anticipating his next bit of dialogue.

"That will prove somewhat difficult, I fear." He cleared his throat. "Gilbert is now committed to marry Miss Morrow."

"Miss Morrow?" Kitty frowned. "The woman who wrote you of Papa's death?"

"How did you know that?" Mr. Wilcox barked.

"When I inquired the circumstances of Pápa's demise, Mr. Glover showed me her letter. He had been reviewing your correspondence, he said, and he wanted to thank Miss Morrow for her consideration, but he didn't know her direction in England—"

"Never mind," Mr. Wilcox interposed. "This is Miss Morrow." He gestured toward Kate, who was still standing in the library doorway. "I should have introduced you earlier."

"Miss Morrow?" Kitty's eyes darted to Kate and widened with amazement. "I presumed you were one of my British relatives. We look a great deal alike."

"So I have been told," Kate said wryly.

"And you are already engaged to Gilbert?" Kitty shook her head with admiration. "You must have won his heart the very moment you arrived."

"Not exactly." Mr. Wilcox cleared his throat again. "The truth of the matter is that Gilbert believes Kate to be you."

"How can that be?" Kitty knit another frown. "Surely Lord Halstead detected the difference."

"I'm afraid not." Mr. Wilcox heaved a deep sigh. "Apparently Glover failed to show you the other letter—the one from your Cousin Jane. Lord Halstead expired a few weeks before Robert, and your Cousin Horace has been dead above a year. Gilbert is now the Earl of Halstead, and your father is, or was, Viscount Latimer. When Kate arrived, she was mistaken for you, and since she fancied you would remain in Virginia, she elected not to set them straight . . ."

He rattled on, but when he finished his explanation, Kitty seemed more perplexed than she had when he started.

"Why didn't *you* set them straight?" she asked.

"And why did you travel all the way to England to notify Papa's cousins of his death?"

"He did not," Kate said. "Mr. Wilcox came to England with the specific purpose of posing as your father."

"Posing as Papa?" Kitty's mouth fell open. "Why should you want to do that?"

"I was thinking of you, my dear," Mr. Wilcox said nobly. "After you eloped, Robert revised his will and left everything to me. His half of the business, the house . . . Everything."

It was possible, Kate conceded. Mr. Sinclair had been prodigious vexed with his daughter.

"And fond as I am of you," Mr. Wilcox continued, "I felt I must abide by Robert's wishes. However, the Latimer estate was an asset he did not know he possessed. I consequently reasoned that if I claimed the title in his behalf, I could, in all good conscience, share the proceeds with you and Thomas."

That was *not* possible. Indeed, his statement was so ludicrous—such an obvious fabrication—that Kate was hard put to quell another giggle. She glanced at Kitty, expecting to see another frown, but Kitty was placidly sipping her brandy. Which, Kate belatedly perceived, was precisely the reaction Mr. Wilcox had anticipated. He had known Kitty all her life, and he must have recognized long since that she did not suffer from an excess of intelligence.

"I understand." Kitty nodded and replaced her glass on the table. "Though it will be somewhat embarrassing when you are compelled to reveal the truth."

"Not embarrassing," Mr. Wilcox said heavily. "It would be *devastating*. For you as much as for Kate and myself."

"For me?" Kitty donned her frown at last.

"Think it through, my dear."

He had used just those words when he was attempting to talk her round, Kate remembered. And how many times before that? Divested of *my dear*, his kind, patient advice to "think it through" had probably lured a thousand unwary business associates into his trap.

"Kate and I should be forced to admit that Robert was the true Viscount Latimer and you are his daughter," Mr. Wilcox went on. "But what advantage would there be in that? Much as we all regret it, Robert is the *late* Lord Latimer. Cousin Jane would undoubtedly take you in, but without a dowry, you'd have no hope of making a good marriage."

He paused to let this dire admonition sink in, and evidently it did, for Kitty's lower lip quivered a bit.

"But if you cooperate," Mr. Wilcox continued, "we shall all reap the benefits."

Cooperate. He had used that word too, Kate recalled. Evidently his repertoire—though exquisitely polished—was somewhat limited.

"Cooperate how?" Kitty said weakly.

Kate was wondering the same thing.

"I fancy the simplest course would be to pass you off as my relative. A relative of Samuel Wilcox's, I mean." He furrowed his brow in thought. "Lord Halstead was aware I'd never been wed, so we shall say that you are my niece. My orphaned niece, whom I bred up and regard as fondly as a daughter."

"But no one knows you are you," Kitty protested. "You are pretending to be Papa."

"Please permit me to finish, dear," Mr. Wilcox snapped. "Yes, everyone assumes me to be Robert, but they also assume Robert's partner is as wealthy as he. We shall say that Kate's splendid match inspired Mr. Wilcox to wed his beloved niece to a peer as well. He sent her—you—to England with that objective in mind, authorizing Lord Latimer—me—to pay a handsome dowry."

"But you said I had no dowry!" Kitty was literally wailing with confusion.

"That is the reward for your cooperation," Kate explained. "If you agree to represent yourself as Mr. Wilcox's niece, he will provide one."

The setdown was growing sweeter by the second, she reflected. With any luck, Kitty would meet a suitable *parti* at once, and Mr. Wilcox would have invested another ten or fifteen thousand pounds in his ill-fated enterprise before Kate exposed him.

"I see," Kitty said dubiously. "You are to pose as Papa"—she looked at Mr. Wilcox—"and you are to pose as me"—she shifted her eyes to Kate—"and I am to pose as Kitty Wilcox."

Stripped to its bare bones, the plot sounded impossibly complex to Kate, but Mr. Wilcox enthusiastically bobbed his head.

"Precisely. It is the only solution, my dear. If you cooperate, you may well end by being a countess yourself. If you do not . . ." His voice trailed ominously off.

"I understand," Kitty repeated. "But how should we address one another?"

It was an astonishingly sensible question, and Mr. Wilcox gnawed his lip a moment.

"In the circumstances we've devised, you and Kate would be lifelong friends," he replied at length. "You'd certainly call one another by your nicknames. And inasmuch as you've always referred to me as Uncle Samuel, I daresay it would be easiest if you now called me Uncle Robert. Can you remember that?"

Kitty eagerly inclined her own head. Her green eyes had begun to sparkle, Kate observed; apparently—now her confusion was resolved and her future assured—she was delighted to find herself engaged in such an amusing game. But could she play her part without a hitch for weeks and months to come? Kate cast about for some way to emphasize the importance of their masquerade, but her thoughts were interrupted by the clatter of a carriage in the street.

"They are back," Mr. Wilcox hissed. "Uncle Robert, Kitty. Remember *Uncle Robert*." The front door creaked open, and he leapt to his feet.

"Luggage?" Lady Latimer emitted a gasp of horror. "Surely Kate is not so ill that she must be removed to hospital." Her footsteps tapped across the vestibule. "There you are!" She sagged against the library doorjamb, fanning her face with relief. "I feared to discover you on a litter . . ." She spied Kitty and sputtered to a halt.

"We have had the most wonderful surprise!" Mr. Wilcox said jovially. "A visitor from Bermuda." He tugged Kitty up and led her to the doorway. "Catherine Wilcox, my partner's niece. This is Lady Latimer, dear."

"Lady Latimer." Kitty nodded, but she was gazing at the rest of the arriving party, who had clustered in a curious knot immediately behind her ladyship.

"And this is Miss Dalton," Mr. Wilcox went on. "A close friend of the family. And my cousin Mr. Sinclair."

"Miss Dalton. Mr. Sinclair."

Kitty sounded peculiarly distant, and Kate realized that her attention was riveted to Gilbert.

"And this is Lord Halstead," Mr. Wilcox concluded.

The earl stepped past Lady Latimer, took Kitty's

hand, and bowed over it, but his eyes never left her face. "Miss . . . Miss Wilcox," he stammered.

"Lord Halstead." Her cheeks colored again. "I do wish you would call me Kitty."

"Kitty?" Lady Latimer echoed. "It is scarcely a wonder that Kate insisted on changing her nickname. Two Kittys in such close proximity must have been excessively confusing. Particularly since they look so much alike."

"That it was." Mr. Wilcox chuckled. "Kitty's parents died when she was quite young, and from the time she came to live with Samuel, she and Kate were inseparable. Samuel and I would invariably yell for one only to have the other appear instead. Eventually, my clever daughter decided to use another name."

"Well, Miss Wilcox would be welcome by any name," Lady Latimer said kindly.

She patted Kitty's shoulder, but her gesture went unnoticed, for Kitty was still staring at Gilbert. The late Lord Halstead had been concerned that she might be taller than his son, Kate remembered, and it appeared to the casual glance that she had the advantage by several inches. But Kitty had never removed her high-crowned leghorn hat, and when Kate made allowances for it, she saw that they were exactly the same height: neither had to look up or down as they continued to gaze into one another's eyes.

"How good of you, Cousin Jane." Mr. Wilcox patted Lady Latimer's shoulder in turn. "Your offer of hospitality is so gracious that I hesitate to request another favor, but I must beg your indulgence even further. Samuel sent Kitty to England with the hope that she might meet and marry a peer. He will provide generous compensation, of course," he added hastily. "Samuel is at least as wealthy as I, and he has authorized me to arrange an extremely handsome settlement. But I shall have to rely on you to take Kitty under your wing and present her to the eligible young men of your acquaintance."

"I shall assist as much as I can," her ladyship agreed, "but I have been out of touch with society myself. After a year of mourning, I am barely puzzling out who is still eligible and who is not. Indeed, I learned just tonight that Lady Pemberton's son got himself engaged to Lady Celia Truscott the very *day* he came down from Cambridge." She made a moue of disapproval, then brightened. "However, I am sure Gilbert and Jeffrey have a host of unencumbered friends. Eh, Jeffrey?"

He was also gazing at Kitty, and he started at the sound of his name. "I beg your pardon?"

"I was saying that you and Gilbert will be happy to introduce Miss Wilcox to all the bachelors you know. Mr. Wilcox sent her to England to find a husband."

"Mr. Wilcox," Jeffrey repeated slowly. "Yes, of course."

His eyes flickered to Kate, and she fancied she detected the hint of a smile at the corners of his mouth. But it faded at once, and she decided her imagination had tricked her. Why should Jeffrey be amused by Kitty's unexpected arrival?

"Then let us get Miss Wilcox settled." Lady Latimer interrupted Kate's speculation. "Unfortunately, there are no spare bedchambers, but I daresay she and Kate will enjoy sharing a room."

In point of fact, Kate could conceive of nothing she would less enjoy, but Kitty was supposed to be her "inseparable" companion. She kept her expression carefully blank.

"Although"—her ladyship frowned—"Barbara's bedchamber is considerably larger than Kate's. It might be best to switch things round—"

"No," Barbara interjected. "I don't mind sharing with Miss Wilcox."

"What a thoughtful gesture, dear." Lady Latimer cast Barbara one of her fond beams. "Is that satisfactory to you, Miss Wilcox?"

"I-I'm sorry?" Kitty tore her eyes from Gilbert.

"We have been remarking that Kate's bedchamber is really too small for two, and Miss Dalton has suggested you share her room. Do you have any objection?"

"No," Kitty murmured, stealing another sidelong glance at the earl. "No, that would be fine."

"Let us get you settled then," her ladyship reiterated crisply. "It's past midnight already, and you must be exhausted from your journey. Perhaps the men will consent to carry your cases. I hate to summon a footman at this hour."

She spun around and sailed across the vestibule and up the staircase, the three younger women trailing in her wake. Evidently the men were dutifully executing her instructions as well, for Kate could hear much puffing and panting and a muffled curse or two as they proceeded along the first-floor corridor and up the next flight of steps. She turned at the second-floor landing, thinking to bid Kitty a courteous good-night. But Kitty was peering over her own shoulder, looking down the stairs, once more watching Gilbert.

13

The strident chime of the mantel clock jarred Kate
awake, and when she sat up and peered across the
room, she saw that it was ten. The clock stopped
chiming, and she cocked one ear grouchily toward
the wall beside her bed. Though she had retired
immediately after she came upstairs, she had been
kept awake for hours by the chattering and giggling
in the adjacent bedchamber. She had been unable
to distinguish Barbara's voice from Kitty's or to
make out more than the occasional word, but
every sentence seemed to inspire a fresh gale of
laughter.

However, no laughter was drifting through the
wall this morning—no sound at all—and this circumstance served to fuel Kate's irritation. Kitty
and Barbara, rich and pampered since birth, were
accustomed to staying up half the night and
sleeping half the day away. Kate, on the other
hand, was accustomed to rising at the very crack
of dawn to tend to Papa or Mrs. Todhunter . . .

But she was being spiteful, Kate owned. It was
not the crack of dawn; the sun had been up for
hours. And a little noise was infinitely preferable
to the alternative of sharing her room with Kitty.
Indeed, the arrangement was ideal: Kate still had
her privacy, and Barbara had apparently found
the friend she so desperately desired.

Kate climbed out of bed and glanced at the
bellpull beside the fireplace, debating whether or
not to ring for Sally. Not, she decided. She had—

if indirectly—endured quite enough girlish prattle already, and she had bathed before Lady Pemberton's assembly. She stripped off her night-clothes, splashed herself in yesterday's water, and donned the apple-green morning dress.

Adams's cold must be worse, Kate surmised when she reached the vestibule, for Taylor, the first footman, was sorting the morning mail. As Mr. Wilcox had mentioned to Lady Latimer, there was no official postal system in Bermuda, and Kate had never ceased to marvel that letters could be whisked from one end of Britain to the other in just a few days. Taylor set a small package on the pier table, and Kate's amazement grew. To think that one could send parcels through the post as well—

"May I assist you, Miss Sinclair?"

Taylor finished his sorting and turned around, peering down his nose so haughtily that Kate wondered how he had managed to identify her. He was obviously much impressed by his sudden—albeit temporary—promotion.

"No, thank you," she said. "I was just on my way to breakfast."

"Breakfast is ready," he assured her. "Should you require any further aid, you've only to ask."

He marched officiously into the library, and Kate could not resist the temptation to creep to the pier table and examine the package more closely. It was six inches square, she estimated, and directed to Jeffrey. A gift of some sort? The script on the wrapping paper was large and uneven, suggesting that the sender was a person of limited education. Kate picked the parcel up and found it surprisingly heavy for its size. What could be flat and square, small yet heavy. . . ?

And what concern was it of hers? She felt a familiar stab of regret. Had she not tarried so long with her communication from Bermuda, everything might have been different. As it was, she could but hope that after she exposed Mr. Wilcox, she and Jeffrey would be friends again. She replaced the package on the table and proceeded to the dining room.

Kate could hear Lady Latimer's voice as she approached the archway, but it was impossible to predict who might be with her. Breakfast was laid out at eight o'clock and left on the sideboard till everyone had eaten, and that—Kate had learned—could be any hour between nine and noon. Jeffrey normally took his breakfast early and departed for Brooks's, but if they had come home particularly late the night before, he might not appear until nine or ten. Mr. Wilcox, for his part, rarely appeared *before* ten. Indeed, now he was "a man of leisure," he had taken to rising later and later: yesterday he had not emerged from his bedchamber till half past eleven. And Barbara was the most unpredictable of all. If she had an appointment with Mrs. Copeland or some other critical errand, Barbara would come to the dining room precisely at eight, but if she did not, she might stay abed until the household clocks were striking midday.

Kate reached the dining-room entry and stumbled to an astonished halt. As she had expected, Lady Latimer was seated in her customary place at the head of the table, but Kitty and Gilbert were arrayed on either side. Kate had assumed that Kitty was still soundly asleep, and except for the morning of their tour, Gilbert had never called during the day.

"Do come in and serve yourself, dear," her ladyship said.

Kate nodded and stepped around the table to

the sideboard. The room had fallen silent, and she was certain everyone was watching her. It wouldn't do to spill anything, and to prevent that embarrassing possibility, she contented herself with two rashers of bacon and a muffin. She turned around and saw that her fears were groundless: Kitty and Gilbert were gazing at one another, and Lady Latimer was peering back and forth between them. Kate turned back to the sideboard but discovered she had little appetite. She poured herself a cup of coffee and bore her meager treasures to the table.

"I didn't think you would be awake." Kate sank into the chair beside Gilbert's and glanced at Kitty, who was situated directly across the table.

"Umm?" Kitty murmured dreamily, tearing her eyes from the earl.

"I meant," Kate snapped, "that I presumed you were still asleep. In . . ." She had started to say *inasmuch as you kept me up half the night*, but she fancied that would be spiteful as well. "In view of your long journey," she concluded instead.

"I was very tired," Kitty agreed. "But also very excited, and when I woke this morning, I couldn't wait another minute to see London."

"And I had exactly the same thought." Gilbert shook his head with amazement. "When I woke, I decided I must take Miss Wilcox on a tour of the city."

"Kitty," she corrected.

"Kitty," he echoed reverently.

They began to stare at each other again, and at length, Lady Latimer cleared her throat.

"Perhaps Kate would like to go with you," she suggested.

"And she is welcome to do so." The earl shot Kate a guilty sideward look. "You would undoubtedly enjoy visiting the Tower and St. Paul's again, and we didn't finish at Westminster Abbey—"

"No!" Kate interposed. "No, thank you. I can see the rest of Westminster another time."

"Then if Kitty has finished her breakfast, I daresay we should depart at once." Gilbert leapt to his feet, strode around the table, and assisted Kitty out of her chair. "It is half past ten already. Indeed, *we* may have to see Westminster another day."

"I shall fetch my hat and gloves."

Kitty raced out of the dining room, the earl trailing behind her, and Kate heard the tattoo of her footfalls on the staircase. It did not appear that either she or Gilbert had even started their breakfasts, much less finished, for the plates they had left on the tablecloth were fairly heaped with food. Kitty's feet tapped down the stairs again, and a moment later, the front door slammed closed.

"Was that wise, dear?" Her ladyship knit a frown of concern.

"What do you mean?"

"I mean, if I may be perfectly frank, that Miss Wilcox and Gilbert seem rather taken with one another. She is an excessively handsome young woman, and your engagement has not yet been announced . . ." Lady Latimer paused, and her face cleared. "But I daresay nothing can happen before my assembly. It is only four days off."

Four days! Kate's hands began to tremble, and she returned her cup to her saucer. Another twelve hours had been chipped away. "I daresay not," she muttered aloud.

"Of course not." Her ladyship sketched a comforting smile. "And now, speaking of the ball, I must go for the final fitting of my gown." She laid her napkin on the table and rose. "Be assured," she added darkly, "that I shall give Mrs. Copeland a proper scold. She won't soon make two more dresses so much alike."

She stalked through the archway, and Kate directed her attention to her plate. But she had lost what small appetite she had, and after choking down one rasher of bacon and a few crumbs of the muffin, she pushed the plate aside. She would have liked another cup of coffee, but if she lingered in the dining room, she was likely to encounter Mr. Wilcox or Barbara or—worst of all —Jeffrey. She stood, hurried into the vestibule, and encountered Lady Latimer instead.

"I didn't think to ask if you'd care to accompany me, dear." Her ladyship was tying the ribbons of her Parisian bonnet.

"No, thank you," Kate mumbled. "I have it in mind to read today."

"Well, as I advised you at the outset, you are free to borrow any books you wish." Lady Latimer waved toward the library. "Till later then."

She tugged on her gloves and sailed out the front door, and Kate continued across the foyer. In point of fact, she had borrowed some dozen books already, but she had finished the last of them the day before. She stepped through the library doorway and—too late—spied Jeffrey standing in front of the window.

"Kate!"

He spun his head. He was holding something in one hand, some object he had evidently been studying in the sunlight streaming through the glass. He hastily thrust it in his pocket, and Kate glanced at the Pembroke table beside him. There was a pile of torn brown paper on the surface and, atop the paper, a small, square box.

"Did someone send you a gift?" she said lightly.

"Gift?" he barked. "What gift?"

"I noticed a package for you in the mail."

"It wasn't a gift." He patted his pocket. "It was an item I had . . . ah . . . ordered."

Kate's respect for the English postal system redoubled. It was evidently a simple matter for tradesmen to distribute their wares throughout the country . . . She became aware that Jeffrey was regarding her in a most disconcerting manner.

"I'm sorry to have disturbed you," she murmured. "I wanted to select a book, but I can wait."

"You have time to read?" Jeffrey's eyes widened with surprise. "I should have thought you and Miss Wilcox would be trading *on-dits* for many days to come. Cousin Robert indicated that you are lifelong friends."

"Y-yes," Kate stuttered. "But Kitty wished to see London this morning."

"Indeed"—Jeffrey flew heedlessly on—"I was astonished when you did not insist she share your bedchamber."

"I could hardly *insist*," Kate protested. "Not after Cousin Jane reminded me that it would be most uncomfortably crowded."

"Cousin Jane also proposed that you and Barbara exchange rooms."

"Yes," Kate gulped, "but that would have posed a great deal of trouble. It was late, and we were all tired—"

"Do you intend to trade rooms today then?"

"I . . . I believe not. I daresay Kitty's things have been unpacked and put away by now."

"I see." Jeffrey nodded. "Perhaps you and Miss Wilcox aren't such good friends after all."

Had he somehow puzzled out their masquerade? Kate's heart bounded into her throat, but she shortly decided he had not. His expression was one of polite curiosity—nothing more—and she seized on the explanation he had provided.

"That is it exactly." She bobbed her own head in agreement. "I shouldn't want it noised about, of course, but the fact is that Kitty and I have not been close in recent years." And that, she reflected wryly, was more or less the truth.

"How ironic," Jeffrey said. "You look so much alike that one would suppose you to be sisters. Is there some blood connection Cousin Robert failed to mention?"

The conversation was rendering Kate exceedingly nervous; she could feel tiny beads of perspiration forming on her brow. A blood relationship would account for her uncanny likeness to Kitty, and she wished Mr. Wilcox had thought to invent one. They could have claimed that Kate's and Kitty's mothers had been cousins . . . But it was too late to make such a claim at this juncture. Gilbert might well ask Kitty the same question, and her answer would be different.

"No," she replied. "Our resemblance is just a . . . a freakish coincidence."

How ironic. She silently echoed Jeffrey's words. She had said the total truth this time—untinged by even the slightest dissimulation—but it sounded wildly implausible. She judged it most perverse that the only innocent aspect of their charade should prove the hardest to explain.

"Well, looks are a strange thing," Jeffrey said. "A child may bear no likeness to either parent but keenly resemble an aunt or uncle or distant cousin. Or, like you and Miss Wilcox, two people with no family connection at all can be as similar as peas in a pod."

"A very strange thing," Kate concurred,

drawing a shaky sigh of relief. Strange or no, his doubts had evidently been satisfied. "Now, if you will excuse me—"

"I thought you wanted to choose a book."

"So . . . so I did." She had lost any remote desire to read, but she dared not arouse his suspicions again. She sped toward the shelves on the front wall of the library, thinking to snatch out the first volume that came to hand.

"Yes," Jeffrey mused, "physical appearances are most peculiar. You and I are an excellent illustration of the mysteries of inheritance. You don't resemble your father in the least, and I am the very image of mine. Cousin Robert noticed the similarity at once."

Kate's outstretched hand froze as she recollected Mr. Wilcox's remark. Had he met the late Alfred Sinclair? He and Robert Sinclair had been partners for thirty years, but Jeffrey's father had visited Bermuda more than *forty* years before. Had Mr. Wilcox been there at the time? If so, he might have joined in some of Robert and Alfred's youthful escapades.

Or he might simply have ventured a lucky guess. Not so lucky, actually: one could seldom go wrong if one declared that an adult child resembled one of his parents. Such a comment was invariably construed as a compliment, and the child would either modestly agree ("I do hope I look like Papa") or modestly disagree ("Though our noses are similar, Mama is much handsomer than I").

But why was she teasing herself about it? Kate relaxed and plucked a book from the shelf. If there were lingering doubts in Jeffrey's mind, let him discuss them with "Cousin Robert." She needn't leap to Mr. Wilcox's defense; he had shown himself prodigious adept at defending himself.

"Yes," she murmured. She turned around and

hurried back across the room, hugging the book to her chest. "He has an excellent memory for faces."

"I'm sure he does." Without warning, Jeffrey's hand snaked out, and his fingers fastened round her free elbow and drew her to a halt. "However, I suspect that in this case, his memory was enhanced by his portrait of my father."

A portrait! Kate chided herself. She had overlooked the most obvious possibility of all. Even Papa and Mama, despite their modest circumstances, had possessed eight paintings of various ancestors and contemporary relatives; Kate knew the number because she had studied the pictures so often. A man of Mr. Sinclair's wealth must have had dozens of family portraits, and Mr. Wilcox would have seen them a thousand times during the course of their long acquaintance.

"The . . . the portrait," she stammered. "I had forgotten the portrait."

"But you remember it now?" Jeffrey said.

Kate hesitated, desperately wishing she knew whether *he* remembered. She fancied she could describe Alfred Sinclair's features well enough: both Lady Latimer and Jeffrey himself had indicated that he looked astonishingly like his son. But had he been painted sitting or standing? Perhaps he had posed on horseback; Jeffrey had also mentioned that he was a splendid rider—

"Do you remember or not?"

Jeffrey's amber eyes bored into hers, and Kate recalled the one wise lesson Mr. Wilcox had taught her. *It is foolish to invest more than one must . . .*

"Not really," she replied. "I remember that there was a portrait of your father, but our whole house was full of pictures. I . . . I—"

"You couldn't tell them apart," Jeffrey supplied.

"Yes." Kate nodded. "That is, no. Since I knew none of the people in the paintings, they all tended to look alike."

She fancied that would put an end to their discussion, but Jeffrey continued to stare down at her, the grip of his fingers relentlessly tightening. What did he want of her? Kate wondered wildly. His leanness was deceptive—he was excessively strong—and he was beginning to hurt her. She was at the point of wincing when he abruptly dropped her arm.

"I'm sure you are anxious to begin your book." He jerked it from her hand and examined the cover. "Adam Smith?" He gazed back at her in disbelief. "*The Wealth of Nations*?"

"I am very interested in economics," Kate said stiffly.

"Economics!" He emitted a sardonic chuckle. "Yes, I daresay that is one of your favorite subjects."

He shoved the book in her hand again, and Kate fled out of the library, across the vestibule, and up the staircase—the bitter peal of Jeffrey's laughter ringing in her ears.

14

Kate woke with her heart pounding against her ribs and a leaden knot of panic in her stomach. She had suffered similar symptoms from time to time in her childhood, when she'd had a particularly vivid nightmare and was not yet certain it had been a dream. But she could recall no nightmares this morning—no dreams at all—and she lay still a moment, wondering the source of her terror. She heard a crash on the floor below, followed by a muffled exclamation of anger, and her heart jumped from her ribs to her throat. The ball. The servants had been waxing the floors and polishing the chandeliers and moving the furniture for two full days. And now it was Saturday, and the final preparations for the assembly were obviously under way.

Kate drew herself shakily up and experienced a wave of dizziness. Perhaps, she thought with a flood of optimism, she was genuinely ill. If so, the announcement of her engagement would have to be postponed . . . She felt her brow and ground her teeth with frustration. Her face was cool, and the dizziness had passed as well. Except for her racing heart and churning stomach, she seemed to be in high force.

That left the weather. It had been wet and unseasonably cold all day yesterday; Lady Latimer had grumbled that the conditions more resembled winter than late spring. If there were to be a sudden blizzard, her ladyship would be compelled to cancel the ball. Kate sprang out of bed and sped to the window, but she realized en route that it couldn't possibly snow on the first of June. Indeed, she saw glumly, tweaking the draperies apart, it wasn't even raining: the sun had returned, and the sky was a cloudless blue.

Kate dropped the curtains and heaved a sigh. She had been grasping at straws, of course—desperately seeking some way to delay the inevitable —but there was none. The last hours were slipping away, and when she woke tomorrow, she would be officially betrothed to Gilbert. She wondered if he planned to give her a ring; they had not discussed the matter. In fact, she reflected grimly, they hadn't discussed much of anything.

Kate trudged to the fireplace, twisted the bellpull, then sank on the bed again. She hoped the earl had sufficient good sense not to *buy* her a ring; they could ill afford to squander their limited resources on such frivolities. But if his mother had possessed an engagement ring, she had undoubtedly willed it to Gilbert.

The seconds and minutes ticked away, and Kate glared at the mantel clock. She seldom rang for Sally, and it seemed little enough to ask that when she did, the abigail should come at once. Kate tilted her head toward the adjoining bedchamber and detected a low murmur of conversation. Evidently Sally was helping Kitty dress.

Kate shook her head with grudging respect. However lacking in intellect, Kitty had proved to be a veritable demon of energy. She and Gilbert had toured London and its environs for four consecutive days, leaving the house early every morning and returning late in the afternoon. Then, despite this grueling schedule, Kitty had floated down the stairs each evening, looking perfectly fresh, and danced till the small hours of the *next* morning. Lady Latimer had sternly cautioned her not to stand up with the same man more than twice, but Kitty had blithely ignored her ladyship's advice. Last night, for example, she had danced with Gilbert at least half a dozen times.

And then—last night and every one preceding—she had come home and whispered and giggled with Barbara another hour or two . . . But it didn't signify. Kate stood up, plodded to the wardrobe, threw the doors open, and irritably examined the contents. Though she didn't intend to leave the house, she was thoroughly tired of her morning dress, and she jerked out one of her walking ensembles.

It took Kate some time to fasten the dress and spencer, and when she examined her reflection in the cheval glass, she was not at all pleased with the result. The canary-yellow spencer—which, Mrs. Copeland had assured her, complemented her dark complexion—now made her appear quite sallow. But that wasn't Mrs. Copeland's fault, Kate conceded. Like most Bermudians, she had spent a part of almost every day outside, and the perennial sunlight had altered her natural coloring. Since her residence in England, her face had paled by several shades, and she really did look rather ill. She applied a generous dab of rouge to either cheek, drew another sigh, and hurried out of her bedchamber and down the stairs.

Kate had planned to proceed directly to the dining room, but there was an impassable barricade in the first-floor corridor. Lady Latimer was raking down three burly men Kate had not encountered before, and Jeffrey was viewing the scene with detached amusement.

"Well, let us ask my cousin," her ladyship snapped. "She is the guest of honor." She turned to Kate. "We were discussing the arrangement of the palms, dear. What do you think?"

She tugged Kate to the drawing-room entry, and Kate peered over the threshold. Adams had recovered from his cold, and Taylor—once more demoted to footman—was sweeping up the shards of a vase and a scattered assortment of crushed flowers. Kate surmised that the crash she had heard was that of the ill-fated vase and that the three strange men were the florist and his assistants.

"What do you think?" Lady Latimer repeated.

Kate gazed around the room. The carpet had been removed and the furniture shoved against the walls, but despite these efforts, there was perilously little space for dancing. And, reducing the available space still further, a potted palm had been situated at each corner of the so-called dance floor.

"I think it would be better to put the palms behind the furniture," Kate replied.

In point of fact, she thought it would be better yet to have no palms. No palms and no dancing. Her ladyship had peevishly remarked that there was insufficient room for an orchestra, but she had insisted on engaging a "small quartet" instead. They were to play in the music room, and Kate was at a loss to conceive how they could all gather round the piano. Unless "small" meant that they were actually dwarfs. But her opinion had not been solicited until this moment.

"That is exactly what *I* think!" Lady Latimer said triumphantly. "Pray see to it, Mr. Perry."

The largest and best-dressed of the strangers clenched his jaws with exasperation, and Kate collected that the palms had been moved numerous times before. But he stalked into the saloon, beckoning his minions to follow, and the three of them picked up the nearest of the pots.

"There is another slight problem." Lady Latimer nervously wrung her hands. "As you know, Cousin Robert and I decided that he would announce your engagement at the conclusion of supper."

Kate knew this all too well: her ladyship and Mr. Wilcox had been debating the matter off and on for days.

"However," Lady Latimer went on, "it now occurs to me that since the guests will be supping throughout the house, only a portion of them would be able to hear the announcement."

She waved one hand vaguely about, and Kate recalled that in addition to the dining room, supper tables were to be placed in the library and both the first-floor parlors.

"So I fancy," her ladyship concluded, "that we should announce the betrothal at the outset of the ball. You and your father and Gilbert can join me in the receiving line, and Cousin Robert can convey the happy news as the guests arrive. Does that course meet with your approval, dear?"

Kate entertained a vision of the scene—she and Gilbert standing side by side, accepting the guests' congratulations—and suffered another wave of dizziness. She shook her head to clear it.

"No?" Lady Latimer said sharply. "What is your objection?"

"I . . . I . . ."

Kate glanced past her ladyship and found Jeffrey's amber eyes riveted to her face. He was wearing his familiar wounded expression, but it was mixed with something else—something she couldn't quite define. Longing? Hope? Her knees weakened, and her heart began to race again, and she realized, with a physical jolt, that she could not go through with it. She still wasn't sure she

loved Jeffrey; perhaps one could never be sure of
such a mysterious emotion. She was only certain
that she could not marry a man for whom she felt
nothing at all. She started to say so, but she owed
it to Gilbert to tell him first.

"I must speak with Gilbert," she blurted out.

"I daresay you should," Lady Latimer agreed.
"He may prefer a different procedure alto-
gether." Fortunately, she had misinterpreted
Kate's words. "But don't dally, dear. You've a long
night ahead, and you'll want to rest this afternoon.
And the coiffeur is coming at four."

Kate nodded and rushed to the end of the hall,
down the staircase, and out the front door. She
had passed Berkeley Square and was halfway to
Grosvenor Street before she recalled that she had
left the house without a bonnet, gloves, or even a
reticule. But it didn't matter a whit: she was so
relieved that she was fairly floating along the
footpath. Though there might be no hope for
her and Jeffrey, it was enough for now that
she was free—almost free—of her obligation to
Gilbert.

And perhaps there *was* hope. Kate was forced to
stop when she reached Oxford Street, and as she
waited for a gap in the carriage traffic, she
remembered the look in Jeffrey's eyes. It was
almost as if he had been begging her to cry off her
engagement. And why had there been no mention
of his own betrothal? Who was to announce that?
Kate had assumed that Mr. Dalton would move
heaven and earth to come to town for such a
momentous event, but—with the assembly less
than twelve hours away—he had not yet appeared.

Kate darted between a curricle and a barouche
and stopped again in the middle of the street. All
things considered, it seemed safe to conclude that
Jeffrey's engagement had, for some reason, been

postponed. So after she talked with Gilbert, she would return to Lady Latimer's house and confess her impersonation . . . She dashed in front of a hackney coach, prompting a most imaginative curse from the driver, and raced on toward Welbeck Street.

Kate had not noted Gilbert's specific direction on the occasion of her previous visit, but his house was readily identifiable by its rusting fence, crumbling pilasters, and the broken pane of glass in one of the second-story windows. She paused on the doorstep, gasping for breath, and belatedly recollected that it was far too early to be paying an unscheduled call. The clock in her bedchamber had struck half past eight while she was dressing, and no more than an hour could have elapsed since then. In view of the "long night ahead," the earl might well be still sleep—

The front door creaked open, and Gilbert blinked down at her.

"Kate?" he croaked. "What . . . what a surprise. I was just at the point of calling on you."

He couldn't be half so surprised as she, Kate reflected wryly. She had expected to be granted a few minutes' grace in which to compose a suitable speech.

"But we can . . . er . . . chat here." He snatched off his beaver hat and ushered her across the vestibule and into the parlor on the right-hand side. "Shall I ring for tea?"

Kate hesitated. Though she would have time to sort out her thoughts while the butler was puttering about, every moment of delay would render her ultimate pronouncement all the more painful. It was surely best to state her message at once and be done with it.

"No, thank you. I shan't take much of your time, Gilbert."

"That remains to be seen," he muttered. "You will sit down at least?"

He gestured to one of the threadbare chairs, and she shook her head.

"No, thank you," she repeated. "I . . . " Her throat closed, and she paused to clear it. "Permit me to begin by saying that I am excessively fond of you."

"I know you are," the earl said heavily. "It is that very factor which makes it so difficult for me to tell you what I must."

"Prodigious fond of you." Kate flew on. "But . . ." She registered his words and once more sputtered to a halt. "What must you tell me?" she demanded.

"That . . . that . . ."

He was twisting his hat round and round in his fingers, and at length, he tossed it on the battered sofa table. It bounced off and rolled back toward him, but he did not appear to notice.

"ThatIcannotwedyou," he finished in a rush.

His syllables had run all together, and another second or two elapsed before Kate divided them into a comprehensible sentence.

"You . . . you can't?" she stammered.

"Please try to forgive me." Gilbert bounded forward, trod squarely on the hat, and smashed the crown almost flush with the brim. "Had I anticipated such a situation, I should have canceled our nuptial agreement at the outset." He contritely seized one of her hands in both of his. "But I didn't expect, after all these years, to meet the woman of my dreams . . ."

He stopped and shook his head in wonderment. "However, that is precisely what happened. Kitty and I have fallen over head and ears in love, and I couldn't possibly marry anyone else."

"You and Kitty?" Kate swallowed an hysterical

peal of laughter. If only Mr. Sinclair were alive—

"You mustn't blame her," the earl said loyally.
"I wanted to announce our engagement this
evening, but Kitty refused. She pointed out that it
would be exceedingly tactless. Like . . . like . . ."

"Like rubbing salt in an open wound?" Kate
supplied, stifling another giggle.

"Exactly." He patted her hand, then released it.
"Though we do wish to post the banns tomorrow."

Kate's amusement evaporated. This was a
complication she had not considered: how her confession would affect Kitty's future. Once Mr.
Wilcox was exposed, he would have no reason to
provide Kitty a dowry, and Gilbert might decide
not to wed her after all.

"Tomorrow," Kate echoed carefully. "Will that
give you sufficient time to arrange a settlement
with . . . ah . . . Papa?"

"I am not eager to bargain with Lord Latimer
again." The earl sketched a grim smile. "Our
negotiations were difficult enough when your
future was at stake, and now I've jilted you . . ." He
visibly shuddered. "No, I shall marry Kitty
without a dowry and rely on her uncle to offer a
fair settlement after the fact."

"I see." Kate bit back a grin of her own.

"And should Mr. Wilcox decline to offer *any*
settlement, I should nonetheless be happy,"
Gilbert continued. "Indeed, I should be happy if
Kitty and I were compelled to live in a garret." He
gazed blissfully into space a moment, then
returned his eyes to Kate. "I hope you don't hate
me too much."

"I don't hate you at all, Gilbert." To the
contrary, her heart was soaring with relief. But
there was no harm in allowing him to believe that
he had jilted her; no one but Jeffrey need ever
know the difference. "I sincerely pray that you

and Kitty will be as happy as you anticipate. Now, if you will excuse me, I must be getting back."

He nodded, then knit a puzzled frown. "But why did you call in the first place? I neglected to ask."

"It no longer signifies." And that, she thought joyfully, was the truth. "Cousin Jane had a question about the receiving line."

"Aunt Jane." He groaned. "She must be told, and your father as well . . ." He bent and plucked up his hat, but it was beyond salvation. "If you'll wait till I fetch another hat, I shall accompany you."

"No, thank you. I am in a monstrous hurry."

"But the burden shouldn't fall on you," the earl protested. "It is my responsibility to break the news."

"I quite agree." Kate's joy bubbled to the surface, and she laughed aloud. "Come along when you can. I promise I shall say nothing to Cousin Jane or Papa either one. I have another matter to attend."

She rushed out of the parlor, across the vestibule, and through the front door. She felt so light that she was inclined to spread her arms and *fly* down Welbeck Street, but she set out at a dead gallop instead.

15

The clock in the rear hall chimed twice as Kate burst into the foyer, and she surmised that it was half past ten. How remarkable, she thought, closing the door and leaning against it. In a mere hour's time, she had walked to Gilbert's, terminated her engagement, and walked (well, *run*) back to Charles Street. More remarkable yet, she was only a trifle winded. After two or three deep breaths, her respiration returned to normal, and she drew herself up and hurried to the dining room. With any luck, Jeffrey would still be at breakfast.

But he was not, Kate saw when she reached the archway and peered around. Kitty was alone, seated on the far side of the table, idly stabbing at a mound of scrambled eggs. She looked up, and her fork clattered onto her plate.

"Kate!" she screeched. "Good . . . good morning."

"Good morning." Kate absently nodded. "Where is Jeffrey?"

"He finished his breakfast a few minutes since and said he had an errand."

"Then perhaps he hasn't yet left the house. If you will pardon me, I need to talk with him." Kate turned back toward the vestibule.

"Now?" Kitty wailed. "I . . . I believe Gilbert has it in mind to pay you a call."

Kate hesitated. She had a clear view of the front door from where she stood; Jeffrey could not depart without her detection. So it was undoubtedly best to conclude her business with Kitty before she proceeded any further.

"Gilbert did have it in mind to pay me a call," she said, glancing into the dining room again, "but I have just returned from calling on him. He explained everything."

"I see." Kitty contritely lowered her green eyes. "I am dreadfully sorry, Kate. I never meant to steal Gilbert away from you, but we fell in love the instant we met—"

"So he advised me," Kate interposed dryly. "He described you as the woman of his dreams."

"He is excessively romantic." Kitty blushed and raised her eyes. "But I didn't tell him of our masquerade," she added hastily. "Uncle Samuel will still give you a dowry."

"No, he will not." Kate shook her head. "I judge it only fair to warn you that *I* intend to reveal our masquerade. That is my reason for wanting to speak with Jeffrey. There will be no dowry for either of us, Kitty."

"Well, Gilbert and I shall make ends meet." Kitty flashed a cheerful grin, then sobered. "But I do wonder what will become of you."

Kitty and Lady Latimer were much alike, Kate reflected grimly: despite their apparent lack of sense, they had a way of cutting matters to the very bone. Her stomach fluttered with panic. She was at the point of violating Mr. Wilcox's cardinal rule—at the point of investing *everything*—and what if she were wrong? She had deduced, on the slimmest of evidence, that Jeffrey's engagement had been postponed, and she might have imagined the look in his eyes. Indeed, she might have imagined that he ever cared for her at all. And if she had, what *would* become of her? No one of any consequence would wed the daughter of a colonial shopkeeper.

"I shouldn't give you away," Kitty said quietly.

How remarkable, Kate thought again. If she were blind and could identify people only by their words, she would never guess that this was the same young woman who had appeared on the doorstep just five days before. That Kitty had been silly and selfish, shedding crocodile tears for her father, and this one was genuinely concerned for another young woman she scarcely knew. Evidently love did, indeed, wreak miracles.

"I'm sure you wouldn't," Kate murmured. "But . . ."

"But you would like to be wanted for yourself," Kitty supplied.

"Yes." Kate nodded; it wasn't too far from the truth. "So if you will excuse me, I shall see if Jeffrey is still here. I wish you happy, Kitty."

What had prompted that comment? she wondered, speeding back into the foyer and up the staircase. It sounded as though she didn't expect to see Kitty again. Which was absurd, of course. Even if she were wrong about Jeffrey's feelings, surely he would not insist that she be evicted from the house.

Kate stopped on the landing and peered warily down the first-floor corridor. It was deserted, she observed with relief, but she could hear a continuing bustle of activity in the drawing room. She crept toward the next flight of steps, and she had successfully passed the saloon when Lady Latimer's voice caught her up.

"There you are, dear." Her ladyship stepped out of the music room. "I am attempting to decide how the quartet should be placed. Do you have any suggestions?"

"Not really," Kate replied. In fact, she judged it likely that one of the violinists would be compelled to stand on the shoulders of the other.

"Well, I daresay Mr. Ingram will think of something. Did you speak with Gilbert?"

"Er . . . yes."

"And when would he prefer your engagement to be announced?"

Never, Kate started to say, but the earl was right on that head: it was his responsibility to deal with his aunt. "He will be calling shortly," she mumbled aloud. "He wishes to discuss the situation with you himself."

"I hope he won't delay." Lady Latimer knit a little frown. "I planned to rest this afternoon."

Kate experienced a familiar prickle of guilt. Lady Latimer truly did have the soul of a saint, and she had been deceived and betrayed at every turn—

"But don't tease yourself about me, dear." Her ladyship patted Kate's cheek. "You're the one who needs rest. I'm sure you fancy yourself too excited to sleep, but if you go to your room and lie down and close your eyes, you will eventually drift off. I shall send Sally to wake you when the coiffeur arrives."

She dropped her hand, and Kate swallowed a sudden, inexplicable lump in her throat. No, not inexplicable, she amended. Her remark to Kitty had been no accident: she was now entertaining the notion that she would never see Lady Latimer again either. Good God. Had she grown as superstitious as Captain Forbes?

"Get along with you," her ladyship said crisply. "The caterer is due at eleven, and I shall have to supervise while his assistants set up the supper tables."

Kate bobbed her head—she did not trust herself

to speak—and proceeded down the corridor. She had composed herself by the time she reached the staircase, but when she turned to offer a polite good-morning, Lady Latimer had disappeared.

Kate stopped again at the second-floor landing, half hoping she had missed Jeffrey after all. If he had departed for his errand, she would have several hours to devise a suitable speech . . . His bedchamber door opened, and he stepped into the hall. He was clearly ready to go out—he was holding a hat in his left hand—but he stood motionless for perhaps five seconds, gazing at the blank wall across the corridor. He was apparently considering whether he had forgotten something, and at length, he bobbed his head and strode back across the threshold. Before her courage could disintegrate altogether, Kate hurried up the hall.

Jeffrey had left his door open, and though Kate certainly hadn't intended to spy, she could not but notice that he was rummaging through his dressing-table drawer. He removed a small object, cupped it in his right hand, closed the drawer, and started back across the room. He was studying the item he'd retrieved as he walked, and she was just at the point of clearing her throat when he glanced up.

"Kate." He said her name without inflection. "I collect you've concluded your chat with Gilbert?"

She had intended to confess her impersonation first, but she judged it best to utilize the opening he'd provided. "Y-yes," she stuttered. "We decided to terminate our engagement."

"Did you?" He chuckled. "In that event, you might be interested to hear what I have decided."

Kate's knees weakened with relief. It was going to be easier, far easier, than she'd fancied. He was going to tell her he had decided not to wed Barbara—

"I have decided to consult my solicitor," he went on. "I shall ask him what legal remedy can be sought in a case of deliberate fraud. The fraud perpetrated by you and your alleged father."

He chuckled again, and Kate perceived that the sound was devoid of amusement.

"You know," she said gratuitously. Her knees weakened further, and she sagged against the doorjamb. "But how . . . when . . ." She tried to moisten her lips, but her tongue was equally dry.

"I am tempted to claim that I doubted your identity at the outset, but I shouldn't want to exaggerate my cleverness." Jeffrey sketched a sardonic smile; he seemed to be enjoying himself. "By the time I met you, Cousin Jane had already explained the confusion surrounding your nickname, and I didn't think to question the matter any further."

"That was an accident," Kate protested. "My Christian name is Catherine—"

"So I subsequently surmised." He waved her to silence. "It doesn't signify in any case. Your name was merely a convenient coincidence. The critical component of the scheme was your astonishing likeness to Kitty Sinclair."

"Yes," Kate agreed. "But I learned of that by accident as well—"

"Though there was some confusion on that head too." Jeffrey forged relentlessly ahead. "Daniel had described a very tall woman with green eyes. However, I subscribed to Cousin Jane's view that his perception was a trifle distorted. Appearances are always filtered through the eyes of the beholder, are they not?"

It was obviously a rhetorical question, and Kate elected not to respond.

"No," he continued, "I first suspected something amiss the morning after your arrival. I could scarcely believe Cousin Robert had never mentioned my father's visit to Bermuda. Another peculiar circumstance arose that night at Almack's, when you indicated you weren't aware that Gilbert stood to become a marquess. And then, the following day, you admitted you knew nothing of Uncle Edwin's voyage on the *Exeter*. As Barbara commented at the time, that seemed prodigious odd indeed."

"Then why did you let it pass?" Kate demanded. "Why didn't you challenge me at once?"

"Because I couldn't be sure, and I . . ." He stopped and bit his lip, as if he had been at the point of saying too much. "I preferred to give you the benefit of the doubt. Indeed, if I recollect aright, I was busily fabricating explanations for the various discrepancies I had noted." He flashed another caustic grin. "I daresay I should still be doing so had your so-called father not arrived. Much as I tried, I could not explain away *his* appearance."

"I don't understand." Kate shook her head. "You never met Mr. Sinclair."

"No, I did not," Jeffrey concurred, "but I had seen his picture. That was the fundamental flaw in your plan, Kate. Cousin Robert and Papa exchanged miniatures while Papa was in Bermuda. Crude little watercolors painted by a street artist; Papa once remarked that they had posed for under an hour. Though I hadn't looked at the portrait in years, I remembered Cousin Robert's most distinctive feature. I thought I remembered, I should have said. I wasn't sure of that either. I consequently wrote to my housekeeper in Hampshire and instructed her to send the miniature to London. That was the package I received, and this is the picture."

He opened his right hand and thrust it forward,

extending his palm so near Kate's nose that she could make out little more than a blur of color.

"What do you see?" he said.

He was speaking rhetorically again, but Kate stepped back and studied the painting nonetheless. As Jeffrey had stated, it was crudely rendered—the white neckcloth and red coat collar merging in a shapeless blob of pink—but it was unmistakably Mr. Sinclair. A much younger Mr. Sinclair, of course: his long brown hair was tied back, and his face was nearly as thin as Jeffrey's. Thin and tanned to a glowing golden hue; the unhealthy flush would come later, after decades of excess food and drink.

"A man can change a great deal in the course of forty years." As Kate had expected, Jeffrey did not await a response. "His hair can gray, his complexion can pale, his face can thicken. But his eyes cannot turn from brown to gray."

Kate was still gazing at the miniature, and she saw that the anonymous artist had perfectly captured Mr. Sinclair's brown-black eyes.

"But I am getting ahead of myself," Jeffrey went on. "The picture merely confirmed my suspicion. I had guessed the night before I received the miniature that the man claiming to be Cousin Robert is his partner, Samuel Wilcox."

"Yes." Kate looked up. "But I did not—"

"I further deduced that Kitty Wilcox is actually Kitty Sinclair. *A very tall woman with green eyes?* It could be no one else."

"Yes," Kate repeated. "But I can explain—"

"I must own that I am somewhat puzzled as to the precise sequence of events." Jeffrey once more gestured her to silence. "I surmise that after Cousin Robert wrote to announce the time of Kitty's arrival, something occurred to alter her plans. Since she appears to be in excellent health, I assume it was a man."

Kate's jaw sagged with astonishment. "How . . . how. . . ?"

"It required no great genius," Jeffrey said dryly. "What else could prompt a young woman to refuse even to meet such a splendid suitor as Gilbert? Had she come to England and found him altogether odious, she could always have cried off. No, she fancied herself in love with someone else and declined to leave Bermuda."

"Not exactly." Kate shook her head again. "In point of fact, she had left Bermuda already. Her suitor was an American sea captain, and she had gone with him to Richmond."

"Ah." He nodded. "That answers my principal question. I had wondered how you and Wilcox concocted your plot without Kitty's knowledge."

"There was no plot, Jeffrey! I did not intend—"

"And now I understand." He flew heedlessly on. "When Cousin Robert died, you and Wilcox believed Kitty to be permanently sequestered in Virginia. It was an easy matter to send you to England in her stead."

"That is not what happened," Kate insisted. "Think it through, Jeffrey." Good God; she sounded like Mr. Wilcox. "At the time I sailed, neither Mr. Wilcox nor I knew of Lord Halstead's death. He would have detected my impersonation in an instant. Indeed, we didn't even know Cousin Horace had died—"

"You *said* you didn't know," he corrected. "It was a clever ploy, Kate; I'll grant you that. The truth was so simple that it took me several days to puzzle it out. But at length, I realized that you could have invented the date of your departure from Bermuda as glibly as you invented everything else. We had only your word that storms and doldrums had extended your voyage to six weeks. The fact is that you left Bermuda a day or two after Cousin Jane's letter arrived and reached Plymouth on schedule."

"No!" Kate croaked. "If you would listen a moment—"

"Which brings me to my second question." Jeffrey frowned. "I still don't understand why Wilcox did not accompany you to England. I can only speculate that he needed time to arrange his business affairs. But that doesn't signify either. Whatever the cause of the delay, he availed himself of the opportunity to review Cousin Robert's family portraits."

"Please," Kate begged. "There was no delay—"

"Unfortunately, Wilcox didn't recognize the significance of the miniature." Jeffrey's lips formed the twisted semblance of a smile. "Evidently Cousin Robert had never told him there was a matching picture of my father. And though that circumstance inevitably doomed your masquerade, I am compelled to wonder one thing more. Why the deuce didn't *you* review the family portraits before you sailed?"

"I have been attempting to tell you—"

"I daresay you were in a considerable hurry." He cut her off again. "That was your mistake, Kate. Your *first* mistake," he amended. "The second was when I asked you about Papa's picture and you pretended to remember it."

"I distinctly stated that I did *not* remember it," she protested. "Not specifically. I recall the conversation very well. It was you who suggested that your father's portrait looked like all the others—"

"But it does not." His voice was patient, almost

kind. "The miniature of Papa is framed identically to this one."

He was still holding the little picture face upward in his palm, and he traced the silver frame with his opposite forefinger. Like the painting itself, the frame was crude; an awkward entanglement of palmetto leaves and some unidentifiable—probably imaginary—vine. Bermuda was famous for its silversmiths, but like any other trade in any other place, there were good workmen and bad. Robert and Alfred Sinclair had obviously closen one of the worst to fashion frames for their portraits.

"I judge it quite hideous." Jeffrey might have been reading her thoughts. "But there is no denying that it's unique. Had you ever seen the miniature, you would have recalled it. You might have forgotten Papa's features, but you would have recollected the size of the portrait and the frame. You could not have confused it with the other pictures in Cousin Robert's house."

He was right, of course, and there was no point in responding.

"I gave you every opportunity, Kate." His eyes had darkened, and he was speaking so softly that she could scarcely hear him. "That is what I started to say before. I didn't want to believe you had deliberately set out to defraud me; I wanted you to confess your impersonation and offer a credible excuse. I briefly fancied you were going to do so the night of Wilcox's arrival, but you did not. You didn't tell me then, and you didn't tell me the next time we spoke in private—at Lady Pemberton's ball. I should have recognized at that juncture that you would never voluntarily admit the truth. But when you blundered into the library and noticed the package, I decided to grant you yet another chance."

He paused, but, again, there was nothing she could say.

"And when you affected to remember Papa's portrait, I still declined to act." Jeffrey shook his head with amazement. "I continued to hope you might confess before your engagement was announced. Indeed, I entertained that hope until this morning, when you went to Gilbert's to discuss the particulars of the announcement. I realized then that you planned to pursue your charade to the end."

"That is not why I went to Gilbert's—"

"But I am getting ahead of myself again." He resumed a normal tone. "The night before I received the miniature, Kitty Sinclair herself appeared. I collect she had some sort of falling-out with her American suitor. You and Wilcox must have been horrified." He emitted another mirthless chuckle. "However, Wilcox swiftly rose to the occasion and persuaded Kitty that it was in her best interest to abet your masquerade. I suspect he convinced her that Cousin Robert had left her penniless and in return for her cooperation, Wilcox would provide her a dowry."

"Mr. Sinclair did leave her penniless. He revised his will after she eloped—"

"Yes," Jeffrey interposed, "Wilcox is excessively persuasive indeed. Which is why I count it imperative to seek the advice of my solicitor at once. I well recognize that a forty-year-old portrait rendered by a street artist hardly constitutes positive proof of fraud. So if you will pardon me . . ."

He made an elaborate bow, dropped the miniature in his coat pocket, and stepped over the threshold. In desperation, Kate reached out and clutched his sleeve.

"Please, Jeffrey," she pleaded. "You have not

permitted me to say a single word in my defense."

"Defense?" He spun around. "What defense? You and Wilcox are impostors, are you not?"

"Yes, but—"

"Then there is nothing more to say."

He shook his arm, as though he were attempting to dislodge an annoying insect, and Kate tightened her grasp.

"There *is* more to say," she insisted. "I did not begin my impersonation for the reasons you think. Indeed, I didn't plan to begin an impersonation at all. I met Mr. Sinclair the night before I left Bermuda, the night before he died. We were to sail on the same ship, and a storm prevented our departure. Mr. Sinclair was coming to England to inform Lord Halstead of Kitty's elopement . . ."

Jeffrey's eyes flickered with impatience, and she felt the hardening of his muscles as he started to shake his arm again. He was clearly in no humor to listen to the whole, complex story.

"I came here with largely selfish motives." She rushed on. "To Charles Street, I mean." With her free hand, she waved vaguely up and down the corridor. "I freely admit to that. It occurred to me that if I took the trouble to inform Lord Latimer of his cousin's death, he might take me under his wing. Lord Latimer, I mean." She was distantly aware that she was repeating herself. "And when Lady Latimer spied me on the doorstep, she mistook me for Kitty."

"And you elected not to set her straight," Jeffrey said.

"I tried to set her straight, but she kept interrupting. You know how she is. So at length, I . . . I gave up. I perceived no harm in it at the time."

"I see. And then—purely by chance, of course— Wilcox appeared, representing himself as Cousin Robert. But you perceived no harm in that either."

"I *did* see the harm," she protested. "I intended
to expose him immediately. But he threatened me
with all manner of dire consequences—"

"No, Kate." His voice was almost kind again, his
expression almost sad. "I have listened to the last
of your fairy tales. Even if I believed you—which I
do not—nearly a week elapsed between your
arrival and Wilcox's. You had ample opportunity
to admit your imposture before he appeared on
the scene."

He pried her fingers from his sleeve, his own
fingers surprisingly gentle, and once more turned
around.

"There was a reason for that as well," Kate
blurted out.

"What reason?" He turned back.

She had not intended to say it, and she gnawed
her lip. But she had lost everything already; she
might as well invest her last figurative farthing.

"I initially continued my impersonation
because . . ." She stopped and drew a shaky
breath. "Because I feared if you knew who I really
was, you'd have nothing more to do with me. And I
. . . I had begun to fall in love with you."

She had not expected that this confession would
inspire him to seize her in his arms and grant
immediate forgiveness; there had been too much
bitterness between them for that. But she had
fancied he would be sufficiently sympathetic,
sufficiently curious, to hear the rest of her
explanation. Instead, he burst into a peal of
mocking laughter.

"In love with me?" he echoed. "Good God, Kate,
do you credit me with no sense at all? Or did you
imagine I'd lived in a vacuum these five days
past?"

"I . . . I don't understand."

"Did you suppose I had failed to notice that

Gilbert and Kitty are mad for each other? Even had I not noticed, Barbara has kept me fully apprised of their blossoming romance. I collect that she and Kitty chat together half the night."

"Yes, they do," Kate mumbled. "But—"

"After our return from the assembly last evening, Kitty advised Barbara that Gilbert planned to terminate your engagement. Barbara relayed the news to me at breakfast this morning, just after you left for Gilbert's."

"Yes, but—"

"There was no *decision*, Kate," he continued brutally. "Gilbert jilted you. Whereupon you rushed back here to claim that you're in love with me. I surmise you chose me as your next suitor because you judged it too much trouble to attempt to charm a stranger."

"That is not what happened!"

"In which case, you did yourself a grave disservice." His amber eyes swept her face. "All else being equal, I daresay you could wrap any man in England round your finger. I have wished a thousand times that we'd met in other circumstances . . ."

His voice trailed off, his eyes briefly darkened again, and then his jaws hardened. "However, that is neither here nor there, for all else is not equal. I expect my solicitor will counsel me to hold my tongue till I have irrefutable evidence of your deception, but I doubt I shall be able to do so. No, should you and your alleged father be bold enough to appear at Cousin Jane's ball, I shall take great delight in publicly exposing you."

"Please, Jeffrey—"

"At that juncture, Wilcox may well elect to engage a solicitor of his own and sue me for slander. It would be the trial of the decade, would it not? Your word and his against Kitty's and mine

—no absolute proof on either side." He grinned with relish, as though he were discussing the prospect of a particularly amusing party.

"Please, Jeffrey," she repeated. "There need be no trial—"

"But I could never allow matters to go so far." His smile vanished as quickly as it had appeared. "I couldn't take the risk of wounding Kitty. I should have to instruct my solicitor to request a postponement of the proceedings and obtain affidavits from Bermuda. Which would not prevent a scandal, of course. To the contrary, the case might drag on for years."

"Please, Jeffrey." Her voice had deteriorated to a ragged whisper.

"But I would win in the end." His eyes narrowed to the merest yellow slits. "Make no mistake about that. If we go to court, I shall spare Kitty as much as I can, but eventually I *will* prevail. Be sure to convey that message to Wilcox, Miss . . . Miss . . ." He stopped and knit a frown. "How odd," he mused. "I do not even know your surname."

"Morrow," she muttered. "Catherine Morrow."

"Miss Morrow." He swept another dramatic bow. "I fancied I'd been trained in all the social niceties, but my instruction did not encompass this situation. I trust you will understand when I say that though I have found our acquaintance extremely . . . ah . . .*interesting*, I sincerely hope I shall not encounter you again."

He clapped his hat on his head, whirled around a final time, and stalked on along the corridor. Kate stood, utterly motionless, as the tap of his footfalls grew ever fainter. At length, she heard the distant slam of the front door and realized she had been holding her breath, waiting for him to race back up the stairs.

No, Jeffrey Sinclair would not encounter her

again, she thought. She refilled her lungs with air and walked unsteadily toward her bedchamber, pausing a moment at Mr. Wilcox's door. She detected a rustle of movement inside the room; apparently he was awake and dressing for breakfast. But she would not convey Jeffrey's warning, she decided. As she had observed all too frequently, Mr. Wilcox was eminently capable of defending himself. She proceeded down the hall and into her own room.

It was clear that she must leave before the assembly, but where was she to go? She still had her letter of credit, and if she were frugal, she could remain in London for many months. She could not live like the daughter of a viscount, of course; she would have to lease a modest little house in an unassuming neighborhood . . .

But to what purpose? She shook her head. She could readily survive without balls and servants and new gowns; she had done so for two-and-twenty years. But every day she stayed in England would be a bittersweet reminder of Jeffrey—the dream that had almost been fulfilled. It was better, far better, to admit defeat and return to Bermuda.

Kate would have preferred to pack in privacy, but her trunk had been removed to the attic the day after her arrival. She sped to the bellpull, intending to ring for Sally. Even empty, the trunk was so bulky that Sally couldn't carry it alone, but she would find a footman and ask him to retrieve it. By the time he completed this task, Kate's smaller case would be ready . . .

Her fingers froze on the handle of the bellpull. And by then, she reflected grimly, word would have circulated all about the household that "Miss Sinclair" was preparing to depart. It was impossible to predict whether Lady Latimer or Mr. Wilcox would be the first to pound on her bedchamber door. Her ladyship—presuming that Gilbert's betrayal had broken Kate's heart—would come to offer solace and beg her to reconsider. Mr. Wilcox would come to rip her out. Meanwhile, the servants would be wearing discreet expressions of pity . . .

No. Kate shook her head again. No, she couldn't bear it. She would pack what she could in her valise and send for the rest when she was resettled in Bermuda. She crossed the room, pulled the valise from beneath the bed, and laid it open on the counterpane.

Her packing for the journey from Bermuda to England had required the better part of a day, Kate recalled: she had painstakingly folded every corset and smoothed every wrinkle from every dress. But now, having determined her course, she was in a monstrous hurry to be gone, and she jerked the drawers from the chest one by one and carelessly dumped their contents in the valise. When she was finished—all her underthings and nightclothes transferred to the case— she calculated that there was space for two dresses. She went to the wardrobe, yanked the doors open, and examined her splendid new finery. She would take no ball gowns, she decided; she wouldn't need ball gowns in Bermuda. She selected two walking ensembles and crammed them into the valise.

And that left only the cloak. Kate returned to the wardrobe, withdrew her threadbare pelisse, and thrust her hand through the tear in the lining. There were more discarded wads of paper than she'd fancied; she had to claw about for some time before she felt Mr. Cottle's envelopes. She plucked them out, carried them to the bed, and placed them in the valise. They were no longer of any use to her, but if she left them behind, Mr. Wilcox might find a way to turn them to his advantage.

That was it then. Kate gazed around the room. As Lady Latimer herself had admitted, it was uncomfortably small, but . . . Well, perhaps Jeffrey had said it best, albeit in an entirely different context. *Appearances are always filtered through the eyes of the beholder, are they not?* Yes, they are, Kate silently concurred, and this little room would always be touched with magic in her memories.

Kate squared her shoulders and closed the lid of the valise. She had laid her favorite new bonnet and gloves on the counterpane, and she put them on, draped her reticule over her arm, lifted her valise from the bed, and carried it to the door. The corridor was empty, and she met no one as she crept down the rear stairs and slipped out the back door of the house.

16

"Miss Morrow?"

Kate glanced up, and Mrs. Rowe, the landlady, beckoned her across the lobby of the inn.

"Yes?" Kate said, stopping in front of the desk.

"Since you are leaving so early in the morning, I must ask you to settle your bill tonight."

"Yes." Kate opened her reticule. "Four shillings, I believe?"

"*Eight* shillings," Mrs. Rowe corrected.

"I understood that the rate was four shillings a night."

"So it is." The ponderous landlady inclined her head, and her multiple chins wobbled in affirmation. "And four shillings a night times two nights is eight."

"But I haven't been here two nights," Kate protested. "I did not arrive till eight this morning, and I shall be departing at half past six tomorrow—"

"An arrival prior to three o'clock is counted as an extra night," Mrs. Rowe interposed. "I have to calculate it that way lest my patrons take advantage of the three daily meals included in the rate."

Kate strongly doubted that anyone would "take advantage" of the meal allowance at the Rose and Anchor; if her breakfast and dinner were representative, the food was quite inedible. But further argument would be futile, she judged, and she extracted a pound note from her reticule. She observed as she passed it across the desk that it was the same note Mr. Barnes had returned to her the day she left Bermuda; she remembered the blob of ink squarely in the middle. It had not made her fortune in England after all, she thought, repressing a bitter laugh.

"Thank you, Miss Morrow." The landlady tendered a scrawled receipt and twelve shillings' change. "I hope your voyage will be a pleasant one."

Bills! Kate stared guiltily at the receipt, recollecting that she had not paid for her new clothes. The bills would shortly be sent to Charles Street, and even if Mr. Wilcox were still there, he would refuse to settle them . . .

But there was nothing to be done about it at this late juncture. It was nine o'clock on Sunday night, and the *Avon* was scheduled to sail at seven in the morning. Ships did not leave for Bermuda every day; Kate had been extremely lucky to book passage so quickly. And—her cash reserve having dwindled almost to nothing—she couldn't afford to wait for the next ship that happened along. No, she would have to instruct Mr. Cottle to forward the necessary funds when she reached Bermuda.

"Is the change wrong?" Mrs. Rowe snapped.

"No." Kate stuffed the receipt and the coins into her reticule. "I was recalling something I failed to do."

"That happens to the most experienced travelers," the landlady said sagely. "I daresay you'll want to be wakened at six?"

"Yes," Kate murmured. "Six would be fine."

She turned away from the desk. She had been exhausted after the interminable, jolting drive from London, and as soon as she'd secured a berth on the *Avon* and consumed as much as she could of her wretched breakfast, she had crawled into bed and slept till early evening. A mistake, she belatedly realized, for now she wasn't the least bit tired. She would grow sleepy again just when it was time to go to the dock.

She sighed and drifted aimlessly out the front door of the inn. Actually, she amended, it was not a *front* door: the main entrance was situated immediately adjacent to the coach yard. But a wide veranda extended round the corner of the building, and Kate strode along the rickety planks, calculating that she would be able to see the harbor from the street side.

And so she could. She sucked in her breath and laid her reticule on the railing of the veranda. The moon was full, and in its brilliant silver light, she could make out the masts of dozens and dozens of ships. The scene was like St. George's harbor magnified many times over, and she thought of her last night in Bermuda. She had gazed out the window of the Palmetto, she remembered, alternately hoping and fearing the storm would lift. If only she had known! If she could have predicted what would happen . . .

No. She shook her head. No, if she were sitting at the same table tonight, the future laid neatly out before her, she would still come to England. She had experienced enough of her dream to sort out what was important and what was not. The trappings meant nothing if there was no one to share them. Gilbert—for all his esoteric prattle— had recognized that fundamental truth before she did. Gilbert had declared that he would be happy to live in a garret if he could live with Kitty, and Kate believed him.

She heard the clatter of a carriage and glanced idly up the street. The vehicle was a chaise, she saw as it raced past the veranda; and the client was either very rich or in a monstrous hurry, for it was drawn by four horses rather than two. In a hurry, she soon decided: the door flew open even as the coach careened into the innyard, and the passenger leapt out before the postilions could rein the horses to a full stop. His features were obscured by a tall beaver hat, but his build and his stride reminded her of Jeffrey.

But it was not Jeffrey, of course; she would never see Jeffrey again. She stared back at the harbor, wondering if she would eventually meet a suitable *parti*. It seemed unlikely, and she further wondered what she would do with the remainder of her life. She had no wish to serve as companion to another elderly widow, and the prospect of governessing was equally bleak. Perhaps Mr. Cottle would help her obtain an interesting post.

There was a thud of running footfalls on the planks of the veranda, and as Kate turned curiously toward the sound, the man she had seen emerging from the chaise hurtled round the corner. He stopped and tore off his hat, and her heart crashed into her throat.

"Thank God," Jeffrey whispered. "Thank God I found you." He tossed his hat on the railing, crossed the space between them, and pulled her into his arms. "Thank God," he repeated, his breath stirring the hair at her temple.

Kate stood utterly still for a moment, too astonished to return his embrace or escape it either one, but at length, she drew away and gazed up at him.

"Am . . . am I dreaming?" she stammered.

"I shouldn't think so." He flashed a wry grin. "If you were dreaming, I daresay you could conjure up a far handsomer fellow than I."

He swept an elaborate, mocking bow, and Kate observed that his appearance did, indeed, leave much to be desired. His hair was tousled, there was a sprouting of beard on his cheeks and chin, and his evening coat and small clothes had degenerated to a shapeless mass of wrinkles.

"I have been on the road since midnight," he said, grinning again as her eyes widened with shock.

"But why?" Kate shook her head. "If I recollect aright, your parting words expressed the hope that you would not encounter me again—"

"And I am sorry for that," he interposed. His smile vanished, and he sighed. "I can but beg you to understand that you had wounded me very deeply."

"*I* had wounded *you*?" Kate said indignantly. "You were the one who—"

"Pray permit me to finish." He laid one finger over her lips, and though his touch was as light as the brush of a butterfly, it set her knees to trembling.

"Finish!" He emitted a sardonic chuckle. "I scarcely know where to start."

"The beginning is normally a good place," she mumbled round his finger.

"Yes, the beginning. I believe I once told you that I doubted the existence of love. Be that as it may, you had a most unsettling effect on me. From the instant we met, I found myself . . ."

He stopped, removed his finger from her mouth, and raked his already untidy hair. "I found myself drawn to you, in a way I hadn't been drawn to any woman before. In other words, it was more than a merely physical attraction. Though that was an element, of course."

He tendered another grin—albeit a trifle shaky —and Kate flushed.

"But I couldn't act on my feelings." He sobered again. "Not so long as you were engaged to Gilbert. I desperately wanted to explain my dilemma, but I fancied even that would be improper. I did attempt to drop a hint the day you returned from your shopping expedition, but evidently you failed to comprehend my meaning."

The matter of honor, Kate remembered. "No, I understood," she rejoined aloud. "Or thought I did. I was at the very point of chasing after you to confess my masquerade."

"Then why didn't you?" His voice was almost a moan. "I would have forgiven you without a moment's hesitation."

"But I didn't know that. I believed I needed time to . . . to win your affection, and I had devised what I fancied to be the perfect solution. I intended to compose a letter, purportedly from Mr. Wilcox . . ." She briefly described her plan. "I calculated that it would kill two birds with one stone," she concluded. "Gilbert had made it clear that he wouldn't wed me without a dowry, and you would receive your inheritance."

"An excellent idea." Jeffrey nodded with approval. "What prompted you to change your mind?"

"I didn't change my mind," Kate said grimly. "I worked on the damned letter for three whole days. That was my mistake. I planned to find it—affect to find it—in Tuesday's post, and Mr. Wilcox arrived Monday night."

"And at that juncture, the letter was useless." Jeffrey bobbed his head again. "But why didn't you simply admit your impersonation? Yours and his as well?"

"Because he persuaded me that you would accept his word above mine. All of you, I mean: you and Gilbert and Lady Latimer and Barbara. As I tried to tell you yesterday, I chatted with Mr. Sinclair only an hour or so the night before he died. Mr. Wilcox reminded me that he and Mr. Sinclair had been partners for thirty years. He'd known Kitty all her life, met Lord Halstead . . . You would believe him rather than me, he said, and you might elect to sue me for fraud. He even threatened to claim I was mad and have me sent to Bedlam."

She expected Jeffrey to laugh at her foolishness, but his jaws hardened with anger instead.

"My poor girl. You must have been terrified." He reached out and stroked her cheek, and Kate's knees began to wobble again. "But after you thought about it, didn't you realize that he couldn't possibly execute his threats?"

"Yes, I did." Her voice was nearly as unsteady as her knees. "I realized it the very next morning, and I intended to . . . to throw myself on your mercy. But before I could, Barbara told me that your engagement—your engagement to her—was also to be announced at Lady Latimer's ball."

"Barbara told you *what?*" Jeffrey jerked his hand from her face.

"She said . . ."

But that was not what she'd said, Kate suddenly recalled. Barbara had said that her father had *agreed* to an announcement.

"She did suggest that possibility." Jeffrey nodded in recollection. "She remarked that Cousin Jane's ball would be a splendid time to announce our betrothal. I used the excuse of my clouded prospects to put her off."

"Put her off?" Kate echoed. "Why was that? You were convinced that I was in league with Mr. Wilcox."

"So I was." He sketched another uncertain smile. "But I had recognized by then that there should be more to marriage than . . . than compatibility. Though I might not be able to have you, I couldn't bring myself to wed a woman who was merely a friend."

He paused and ran his fingers through his hair again. "And it increasingly appeared I could *not* have you," he resumed, "because Wilcox was busily negotiating the terms of your dowry with Gilbert. I collect that it—the dowry—was also the reward for your cooperation."

"Yes." Kate inclined her own head. "And since I believed you'd decided to marry Barbara, I fancied it was in my best interest to marry Gilbert. But I didn't plan to let Mr. Wilcox go unpunished. No, I plotted my revenge very carefully. As soon as my dowry was safely in Gilbert's hands, I intended to reveal our imposture. Preferably in full view of the entire *ton*."

"Kate." Jeffrey clicked his tongue against his

teeth. "I am beginning to fear you are irreparably wicked—"

"But I realized yesterday morning that I couldn't go through with it." It was too soon to joke, too early to laugh away all the pain between them. "That is why I went to Gilbert's, Jeffrey. Not to discuss the particulars of the announcement, but to tell him I couldn't wed him. He literally snatched the words from my mouth, and I perceived no harm in allowing him to think he had jilted me. You can believe that or not."

"I believe it."

He regarded her in silence for a time—a few seconds, half a minute; Kate could not be sure. Then he stepped forward and took her in his arms again, and her mind went altogether blank. She was aware of nothing but the beat of his heart against her and the warmth of his lips on hers. His mouth was gentle at first—once more like the touch of a butterfly—but it soon grew hard. No, not hard. Demanding, insistent, hungry—never hard. She coiled her own arms round his neck and strained against him, parted her lips and felt his tongue. His mouth moved to her ear, her neck, and she began to think again. Passion could not resolve their differences either.

"Why did you not believe me yesterday?" she said. "What happened to change your mind?"

"Must we discuss it now?" he murmured.

He raised his lips to hers again, and she jerked away.

"Yes, we must, Jeffrey. We absolutely must."

He sighed with regret and reluctantly released her. "I went from my solicitor's office to Brooks's and did not return to Charles Street till half past six. Cousin Jane was in a terrible state. Gilbert had arrived at the same time as the caterer, stating that he needed to speak with her and Lord Latimer both. Cousin Jane directed him to confer with Cousin Robert while she dealt with the caterer, and an hour elapsed before she talked to Gilbert herself and learned that he had terminated your engagement. She rushed right up to comfort you and discovered you were missing. Since your clothes were still in the wardrobe and your trunk in the attic, she fancied you had merely gone out for a walk. But you had been away for above six hours by then, and she was beginning to fear that something dreadful had happened. To make matters worse, Cousin Robert had disappeared as well, and she couldn't discuss her concern with him. It had even occurred to her that you might have committed suicide."

"Oh, dear." Kate felt a familiar stab of guilt.

"I put her mind at ease. I said that naturally, in the circumstances, you would wish to avoid the ball. I didn't tell her I had specifically warned you not to attend the assembly. I assumed you had conveyed my warning to Wilcox and the two of you had repaired to a hotel for the evening. But when I went to the saloon at nine o'clock, there he was—all rigged out in his evening clothes and looking quite as smug as ever."

"And you immediately announced that he was an impostor."

"No." Jeffrey shook his head. "My solicitor was very definite in that regard. He pointed out that if Wilcox was aware of my intentions, he might prevail on his friends in Bermuda to supply false affidavits attesting to his identity."

"So you said nothing?"

"No, I didn't have *that* much self-control." He flashed another grin. "I remarked that he must be most distressed by the recent turn of events."

"And he didn't understand what you meant," Kate said. "Because I had *not* conveyed your warning."

"So I later surmised. At the time, however, I thought he was *pretending* not to understand. He replied that I must be referring to your engagement. And while the turn of events was certainly disappointing, he said, there was the consolation that Gilbert had decided to wed his dear partner's beloved niece."

"Good God." Kate could not repress a giggle.

"Good God indeed." Jeffrey's jaws hardened again. "At that juncture, I could hold my tongue no longer. I told him it was futile to continue his game because I knew very well that Kitty Wilcox was actually Kitty Sinclair, that you were Catherine Morrow, and that he himself was Samuel Wilcox. I had a picture to prove the latter, I said, and I would instruct my solicitor to initiate legal proceedings the first thing Monday morning."

"Good God," Kate repeated. "What did Mr. Wilcox say then?"

"He said no legal proceedings would be necessary. I suspected he was perpetrating another trick—putting me off my guard while he pondered his next move. But he went on to say that he knew when to abandon a poor investment. And in this case, he added, he had invested almost nothing: only his travel expenses. Indeed, if the truth had to come out, he was delighted it had come out now, before he expended twenty or thirty thousand pounds on dowries."

Jeffrey shook his head with amazement, but Kate was not surprised. No, had she thought on it, she could have predicted Mr. Wilcox's reaction. Much as he might fancy the notion of being a peer, he would not invest another moment of his time or another farthing of his money in an enterprise which had become so dubious.

"What did you say after that?" he asked.

"To be honest, I was temporarily speechless." Jeffrey sketched a rueful smile. "But at length, I recovered myself a bit and mumbled something to the effect that he really should compensate you for your efforts. Not thousands of pounds, of course—not a dowry. But you had been his coconspirator for many weeks, and you were surely entitled to a salary."

"And he laughed," Kate said.

It was a guess, but an educated one, and Jeffrey nodded.

"Yes, he laughed. You were hardly a coconspirator, he said. Quite the reverse, in fact. He had never laid eyes on you till he arrived in Charles Street, and from that moment on, you had caused him no end of trouble. Far from giving you a salary, he would decline even to pay for your clothes." Jeffrey stopped and once more raked his fingers through his hair.

"And then?" Kate pressed.

"And then I also began to fear that something dreadful had happened to you. As I mentioned before, I had presumed that you and Wilcox were together. But he was with me, in Cousin Jane's drawing room. Where were you? It was almost ten by then. I didn't believe you were the suicidal sort, but if you were wandering round London in the dark . . ."

He shuddered. "It is an excessively dangerous city, Kate. There are neighborhoods so different from Charles Street and Leicester Square that you would fancy you'd been transported to another planet. If you had stumbled into the wrong place at the wrong time, you might well have been attacked. Merely robbed if you were lucky. If not, you could have been raped, beaten, strangled, slashed to ribbons with a knife . . ."

He closed his eyes, as though he couldn't bear to visualize the scene, and Kate reached out and took his hand.

"But I wasn't," she said softly.

"No." He opened his eyes. "But I didn't know that at the time. I raced up to your bedchamber, hoping to find some clue that you were safe. The name of a hotel, the direction of a person you might have been referred to . . . But the top of the desk was bare, and the drawers were empty. And as Cousin Jane had told me, your clothes were still in the wardrobe. Eventually, in desperation, I opened the drawers of the chest and discovered them empty as well. I realized then that you must have had another case in addition to the trunk. Had it, packed it, and left forever. And I had no idea where the deuce you'd gone."

"Then why did you come to Plymouth?"

"They would say at Brooks's that I was hedging my bet." He peered at the harbor a moment, then looked back at her. "I calculated that if you were still in London, I could find you. Indeed, if you were still in *England*, I could find you. It might take considerable time, but sooner or later, I'd track you down. In fact, I could find you even if you returned to Bermuda; I'm given to understand that it's a very small place. But what if you'd decided to resettle somewhere else?"

He crushed her fingers in his. "You might be bound for America or Canada or Australia, and then I would *never* find you. I could only pray that wherever you were going, you would sail from here." He waved at the dozens of masts in the moonlight. "So I borrowed Gilbert's curricle and drove to the Bull and Mouth. It was midnight

before I could engage a chaise to drive me on to
Plymouth, and I've been on the road ever since."

He dropped her hand and stroked her cheek
again. "I still don't know if I love you, Kate. I've
denied the existence of love so long that I'm not
sure what it is. I only know that when I feared I'd
lost you—lost you forever—I couldn't bear the
prospect of living without you."

Was there a better definition of love than that?
she thought. It didn't signify what he cared to call
it.

"So if . . . if you can find it in your heart to
forgive me," he stammered, "I should be honored
to make you my wife."

He sounded as stiff and awkward as a schoolboy
suffering the pangs of his first *tendre*, and Kate
laughed aloud.

"Yes, I'll marry you," she said. "And I daresay
you will come to find me quite *compatible*."

He pulled her into his arms again and kissed her
—very gently this time—then rested his own cheek
against her temple. Kate wished that Mr. Sinclair
could know what he had wrought. Well, perhaps he
did. Perhaps he would be present in spirit when
she and Kitty floated down the aisle of St.
George's, Hanover Square. Lady Latimer, having
staged *two* grand weddings in rapid succession,
would be quite beside herself with pride . . .

"It seems a trifle unfair," Kate murmured.

"What seems unfair?" Jeffrey sighed with
contentment.

"That Barbara should be the only one to suffer."
Kate stood away a bit and gazed up at him. "She's
not a bad person."

"Not a bad person at all," he agreed. "As I told
you at the outset, she is a very pleasant young
woman. But you needn't tease yourself about
Barbara; she won't suffer for long. With all her

father's money, she'll soon find a perfectly splendid husband. Indeed, now I think on it, I realize that I am making a considerable financial sacrifice by wedding you instead of her."

"Jeffrey!" Kate shook her head with mock reproval.

"And Barbara won't be the only one to suffer," he went on. "I neglected to report the conclusion of my conversation with Wilcox. He told you and Kitty that Cousin Robert had revised his will, but I knew that was impossible. Evidently Cousin Robert recognized Wilcox's character all too well, for he composed the will a few weeks after he married and sent it to Papa for safekeeping. It specifies that upon Cousin Robert's death, his fortune is to be equally divided among his wife and any children of the union."

"That isn't unusual," Kate said.

"No, but there is a most unusual provision. Cousin Robert also specified that the will could not be changed unless he advised Papa or Papa's heirs of an intention to change it thirty days before the fact. I had received no notice of such an intention, and when I mentioned that to Wilcox, he admitted that insofar as he knew, Cousin Robert had contemplated no revision. The estate can't be settled for months, but I estimate that Kitty will ultimately inherit nearly a quarter of a million pounds." He frowned. "If I were the least bit sensible, I should try to marry *her*."

"Jeffrey!"

"But I shall settle for you."

He kissed her nose and then her mouth, and his attentions were beginning to grow most serious when they were interrupted by the clatter of a coach pounding into the innyard. Kate glanced grouchily over her shoulder and saw that it was another chaise. She started to turn back to Jeffrey, but at that moment, the passenger alighted, and she recognized Mr. Wilcox. He, too, looked much the worse for wear, she observed: his neckcloth had long since wilted down the front of his coat, his breeches were plastered to his plump legs, and he was fanning his face with his *chapeau bras*.

"Do you see him?" she hissed. "Do you see?"

"Yes, I see," Jeffrey whispered back.

They giggled like two mischievous children as Mr. Wilcox trudged disconsolately into the inn.